BY ALL
OUR
VIOLENT
GUIDES

C.E. YOUNG

A Narmer's Palette Publication

By All Our Violent Guides

Mail comments and requests for permission to
c.edward.young@gmail.com

Narmer's Palette Books

Edmonton, Alberta Canada

Published in the United States of America.

Print ISBN 978-0-9877039-4-1

First Edition, October 2013

Cover design by Nathaniel Hébert,
www.winterhebert.com

For the late Professor Samuel Astrachan, who by now has most certainly and perfectly described heaven.

Thank you, sir.

"One does not place a lounge chair on the Serengeti."

Wise counsel no matter the source.

Part 1
"alone"

One Hour for Lunch

It's hard to give a shit these days.

She danced naked.

She danced naked with a particular scarf around her neck one midnight, footing through a well-lit apartment, unaware a woman across the street had seen her and called her boyfriend in for a look. Living so far off the ground fostered notions of invisibility. Not quite a voyeur's dream, she usually closed her blinds, Regina usually kept clothes on, she rarely danced. When she danced it was in a way no one would admirably recognize as such. But sometimes, particularly summer nights that stretched as far as God could see, she forgot, and danced puttering with cleaning or if she couldn't sleep.

The scarf. Nomo High School. On a whim. It was cold enough outside for a little chivalry. "Give it to me," she said. He was her best friend.

Dead now, died right out of college like a track star winning that last one for the Gipper, collapsing two seconds after crossing the finish line to beautifully ensure the last thing heard was a burst of cheering suddenly swallowed by an absolute and fulfilling silence. Except he was in an idling car at a fatal intersection, and traffic sometimes won't wait that long.

Years ago. That particular scarf was long past trying to keep cold at bay. Its fabric fuzzy, color dull brown, general texture dotted with piles like spider eggs. She tugged it tighter around her lower jaw and tucked it a fold deeper into her collar. Winters were so rough now, so personal.

Regina entered the library stomping snow from her boots, glad the heat was up full blast. The library staff didn't know Regina, she didn't know them, and the three college students inside were so focused she could have been naked for all the attention they paid her. She settled at a table, losing layer after layer of protective wear. Last night a nature program the networks drag out if ratings are a foregone loss had featured an extended segment on oddities of nature and other weird animals too intriguing to eat. One night she had stared out her window—she might have been ten or eleven—and saw very clearly on the roof of the house across the street a small, agile animal with a thin prehensile tail, either white skinned or with very fine, smooth fur. It was about the size of a little boy, and at first she figured it had to be the obnoxious boy who lived there, naked on the roof (at the time, being a lonely little black girl, she believed, based on observational study, that most white children, i.e. little white boys, were handed free run over the earth)—until in one bound it went from the house's crumbling shingles to the chimney to over the dark side where things that had *been* became gone.

Likely somebody's illegal monkey had escaped. White people could own anything, and things always got away. A spider monkey. Except, as she sat in the library reading through *Sumner's Guide to Primates*—it was Saturday; she had all day to satisfy whichever idle curiosity came up—she was informed that the largest species of spider monkey rarely hit more than twenty-five pounds. Lengthwise, two feet of head and body with another two to three of tail were all they could expect of life.

Satisfied she hadn't completely forgotten this personal mystery and being wrong just enough to keep it alive, Regina continued flipping, pausing at a section describing a species of primate that commonly practiced, as essential political tool, homosexuality, male and female, adult and minor.

They were remarkably well ordered.

She had to take that book out. She folded the tip of the page before making her way out of science and into culinary, culinary being the proper reason for venturing out on a wintry weekend to the library in the first place. Regina Nevills was an information junkie. On a budget. Dennis would be over tomorrow night; it was their first apartment-cooked meal together. For five weeks they had dated and dined in ethnic eateries designed to show how cosmopolitan each was. It was time one of them stepped up to bring it home.

She found the perfect cookbook, fat pages full of recipes close to religious experiences they were so full of soul. "Been a while," she muttered at the ingredients, but knew she could whip up genuine soul if seriously motivated. Dennis was a good man. Definitely motivation.

She imagined the appetizers, the sweet potato wedges, honey-buttered cornsticks, warm, fragrant garlic monkey bread that got pulled apart like ripe fruit and popped in the mouth before it got away. Foods like snap bean salad and glazed citrus chicken, none of which she'd ever had or made, but were so much like what home was supposed to be that she felt safe imagining them in her kitchen. A kitchen needed to be a place that meant something, shrine or holy temple, young or old. So far, few kitchens had ever meant that to her. Ma never cultivated the magic.

But the younger Nevills, throughout her adult life, tried in various ways to beat away the prospect of dying without at least once coming close to the taste of home. Regina wasn't old. Actually she was young, her caramel skin free of stipling, spots or protusions; despite that fact there were times she felt so fixed in time, space and circumstance she felt ancient. But she had finally learned to recognize illusions. She was thirty-eight.

Virginia Scott Library kept a bank of public copiers. She liked the sanctioned noise of the machines that made the monastic students glance from their studies. She copied several recipes and left. In the grocery store mothers converged to air their cold, squalling children out. Saturdays were always packed. The aisles were too close together. No matter where Regina turned, harsh words bounced off a kid's head. She wound her cart between adults and children, humming Sam Cook tunes, taking measured breaths, restricting her peripheral vision, just to give all the noise a space where it would fit.

"You damn well better appreciate this," she muttered while in line. "Jesus, is *everybody* unhappy with their kids?"

To which the woman ahead of her turned around to say, and say clearly, "Fuck you," without missing a beat telling her son he'd best shut his little ass.

"Excuse me?"

The woman rolled her eyes and turned away.

"I wasn't talking to you."

"Well I heard you," said the mother.

Regina gripped the cart, ready to ram it forward hard enough to sever the cow's spine. *I'll pray for your idiot soul,* she thought. As the line moved, the woman instantly forgot the exchange. She inched her cart and stopped, inched and stopped, until getting to the checkout to pile the load onto the conveyer. Regina didn't bother counting; of course the cow had more than the lane limit, and had entirely forgotten that Regina was even behind her. The two older kids wisely waited for the youngest to give up asking for things he wouldn't get. They held close to the sides of the cart like inmates, just waiting for the chance to hope to get the hell away from this wombless prison. Regina tried to smile at one of them, peeping at her through the cart's lattice. Mother might've been twenty-one going on twelve, but he was a cutie. This cutie wasn't bashful though. He met her eyes dead on. He stared at her. He let her know: she was of no use to him at all.

She glanced away.

Mother's groceries totaled more than she carried. "How much of these can I put on my food card?"

The cashier asked, "Where'd you get your hair done?" while waiting for Ma to decide which items to put back.

The girl smiled; the tip of her tongue showed at the corner of her mouth. "Shit, seventy dollars up at Nelson's. You gotta get there early though."

"They did a good job."

This hair was a pile of spirals sitting atop her head a good eight inches high, jet-black and blond, looking like an aluminum Christmas tree after a thorough house fire.

The littlest boy whined toward the candy. The woman ignored him, picking through her load for children's items.

Regina wanted to be home. She wanted to be *home*.

And on the way she wished a fervent mortal curse on that woman with the fake Christmas hair.

And each time a car rode her or cut her off she bit hard on that same curse to make it bleed.

Twelve dead people by the time she pulled into her parking space. By the time she locked the door of her apartment she no longer felt she deserved her own name.

"*Sumner's Guide to Primates*," Dennis read, head back and squinting to find the right focus. His glasses were in easy reach. "You're researching my sisters?"

"You can be too silly sometimes."

"You just found this out?"

She plopped next to him, asking, "Did you want to watch the news?"

"Not especially--"

Regina already had the remote aimed. The TV came on. They both assumed the proper quietude.

"...to additional sweeping cuts in social services were attacked outside the State Capitol building by a man carrying pepper spray. Witnesses say the man, who the News Hawks learned carries a recent arrest for aggravated assault, approached the small crowd of protesters as they chanted for legislative unity and compassion, shouted, 'I'll give you something to cry about,' and immediately began spraying, injuring three directly in the face before being wrestled to the ground by two of the protesters until security arrived. One of those taking the full brunt of the attack was a fifteen year old girl who had hoped to deliver a message of hope...to the governor."

Regina flipped channels. At the top of the news hour all the stations hawked the same story. Channel Nine reported the alleged attacker had been recently fired from his job, which led to some confusion as to his message. Eight's stand-in anchor solemnly read that the victims had been treated and released, but that the attacker, Robert Michilane, remained hospitalized with a fractured collarbone.

TV-Four segue-wayed from this story to a commercial for an aging actress' perfume. Then a commercial for meat.

Regina sighed. Crazy had become the order of the day. She thought of what her ideal home would be like.

"Where do they come from?" asked Dennis.

"I wish I knew. I'd charter a boat to their little island and just beg '*Please*, please please.'"

"Do like James Brown."

"Do like with a big ass stick and the right hand of God. You know nobody speaks common sense anymore."

Really wanting her to kill it now, the television, Dennis responded, "Might as well kill it after the weather," kill it, set the remote on the table with a cool and knowing look in her eyes, then ravage the living hell out of him.

He furrowed his brow. What was a law firm receptionist doing with a book on primates?

Robert Michilane, for information's sake, made the news again three days later by escaping custody. How far, if long distance was his destination, could a frantic man with a neck brace go?

Just my luck, Regina thought, *I be the one he runs into*.

At 9:27 a.m.

"Law offices."

"Somebody called me?"

She didn't recognize the voice. He didn't offer to help; the first such call of the day; the day was so young. "I don't know, sir. Do you know of anyone who would be calling you from the law office of Ganos, Opply and Dawn?"

"Is there a Ganos Opply there?"

Caller ID is evil, she scribbled on her note pad. "No, sir, that's the firm name."

"Can you read me some names off?"

"Sir, there are over fifty people here. Do you have a case with this firm?"

"Yeah."

Please?

"What's your name?"

"Hold up, I got my attorney's name right here. Mary, will you gimme that? That paper over there! One all folded up. OK, um, is there a Harold, what's this last name, Niwitski?"

"Nivotoska."

"Yeah, that's it, shit," he gave with a laugh.

"Harold Nivotoska is your attorney," she said flatly, hoping he'd follow a brief example of a thought process. "You've spoken with him at this number before?"

"Yeah, I called his secretary yesterday."

She held her breath much too often at this job. Workplace apnea. "One moment, please." Her fingers flew to send this man away. Daily life didn't let folks get to the post stage. It was ongoing-traumatic stress disorder.

An interoffice line flashed.

"Front desk."

"Regina, could you tell Atefeh to call me?"

She glanced at the display. Gerald Opply was calling from his office. "Certainly, Mr. Opply." Of course Opply hadn't bothered directly trying Atefeh's extension. It would undermine his role as supreme managing partner who had more important things to do than memorize office extensions that hadn't changed for years. Atefeh, the associate whiz Opply'd taken as his personal protégé, was, as she had been for the past two years, at her desk, a personable woman intentionally funny in her struggles not to become too Americanized.

"Mrs. Al-Redin," she formally inquired.

"Ms. Nevills."

"Gerald Opply would like to hear your sweet tones."

"Did it sound important this time?"

"Probably urgent."

"Really?"

"Never." Suddenly three red switchboard lights flashed simultaneously. "Gotta go."

She took a deep breath.

By the time lunch renewed her faith she'd already overheard the operations clerk suggest to three secretaries, subtly and roundabout, that maps to hell were in good supply; overheard Peter Ganos' bassoon voice imploring Gerald Opply to stop being an asshole, it was better if the breakroom's floor remained tile instead of wood, dammit, and if he thought they were going to waste any more revenue on additional half-assed renovations…

It was bitterly cold outside, too cold to be going out, except she hadn't brought her lunch. There was no way in hell that the one hour she had for peace and quiet be devoted to hearing office politics and illness information exchanges in the coffee room. Victor, the "operations clerk" as he'd titled himself, usually headed out the same time she did. Of employees who addressed her as Ms. Nevills, he was the only one did so with a hint of actual deference. Whenever he held the door for her he nodded and said her name as she passed. He always reminded her of a young man, forlorn, privately seasoned into an army of one. On the elevator ride down with him she decided it was time he had lunch with her.

When the wind blew harder he walked closer beside her.

In the restaurant Victor Robbins discretely watched Regina chew. Fork to mouth, fork inside, lips close, fork slides out. It wasn't nice torturing him like that but he was cute. Would've been sweeter if she'd had voluptuous lips, but he struck her anyway as the kind of man who would never fall in love with a face from a magazine. She felt wicked pride knowing tonight someone might stare at the ceiling thinking about her lips.

"Why the smile?" he asked.

"Good mostaccioli. You never talk much, Victor."

He shrugged. "Ain't enough up there know how to listen."

"Never gone to lunch with anybody either."

"With reason."

She waved her fork as prompt.

"I don't chew with anybody thinks I need a highchair one way or another."

"How old are you?"

"Twenty-three. You?"

"Thirty-eight."

His appreciation rose.

"How long up there?" he asked.

"Eleven years."

"Eleven years," he repeated. He chewed a spoonful of chili thoughtfully.

She chewed thoughtfully too. "I might take some classes," she said.

"Community?"

"Simpkins. Where you got your bachelor's? You might not talk much but I do hear."

"What's it in?" He actually had dimples when he smiled. If he'd been older she might've entertained, simply to give a few neurons something to do, the half-wit notion of taking him to bed.

Or the supply storage room.

She cleared her throat.

"Don't know."

"Life."

"Biology?"

Victor glanced at his watch. "Sociology."

"So what're you doing as a runner?"

Hope seemed to drain from him without her noticing it had ever been there. "Paying bills."

On the elevator back to the office (twenty minutes late) she asked if he might use her first name now. He answered that some cultures considered eating together a particularly intimate experience, more so than sex. His eyes were glued to the numbers lighting up one by one. With each floor he wished that the usual impediments to paradise faded out of existence and at their floor they would exit at a garden. Her perfume smelled like roses. Not the thick, sugary scent usually captured in glass tubes, but the real thing, tinged at the edges of perception with chlorophyll and soil. Roses gently filled the elevator box, getting into his hair, getting into his clothes. "Know what?" he said. It was comforting the way he noticed his attraction to her without her even trying. "You made a friend today. Not that I never liked you before--"

"You'll let me know when it's time to meet your parents?" she said. He smiled and looked away. Victor Robbins was bashful!

She wanted to hug him like a son.

Stepping off the elevator, she stopped him at the office door and thanked him.

He opened the door for her. "You're all right, Regina."

"Not too many of us inkspots in here," she said safely. "You with me?"

"I'm with you, my Nubian sister." Although, visually, she was more a smudge than a spot.

With you, he'd agreed, *but with you in what*?

They went back to work.

2

Backfield in Motion

He hadn't said a word since the moment the first button came undone. Hadn't picked his coffee up. She had more than Dennis' attention, she had his gratitude and utmost respect for not marring this sensual display with gaudy, sexless caricatures.

Blouse came open. She twisted an arm so she could unhook her bra, but she didn't pull the bra out. She let him watch the weight of her breasts take the fabric, dropping the cups outward a single heartbeat.

She hadn't uttered another sound except his name after returning to the cozily lit living room where he sat. Where he thought after she came out of the bathroom she would simply resume the conversation. He looked up at his name; she undid the top button (he froze) using both hands at the plum-soft hollow of her throat.

Without pause she undid the second in the same fashion, using both hands. Then the third with her left hand, the fourth her right. He wasn't sure when the blouse came out of her pants; after that fourth button he noticed these two things: Regina's hard olive eyes. They caressed his face but yielded no ground. Involuntarily, he swallowed staring into her eyes. In them a combination of lust and determination told him he was going to make this first time love with her, and no one but her, in this place at this time, not his first crush, lost love, ideal mate or feminine gestalt. And when it was over, whether he was asleep or not, *she* would remain.

A hunt for love required all or nothing.

Light from the television skated across his glasses. His seated angle was just right for a televised image to jump at her here and again. Behind her the box's volume attempted to draw attention.

"Donho," said the battered hero, "how fast can you get to Santa Magreta? No, she is not dead... Donho? Pack for cold weather. Bring your special friend."

Brash guitar music heralded a sequence of action cuts, then came the drums, the primitive action sequence drums.

Blouse hanging open, pants untouched, Regina left. She knew Dennis' bedroom was somewhere left of the television.

And assumed he would know where to find her.

...*So Ma*, she jotted as that night settled into Wednesday morning, *been two months of the coldest winter I can remember. I'm ready to move. How you doing? I know it's been a while. Sorry.*

Sorry.

Sorry was too big a speed bump.

Outside, the one a.m. wind calmed a moment. Winter became a snap shot.

She regretted not staying the night. Thinking about Dennis led to wanting to write Ma, share a bit of good news after so long, two, three months out of touch.

With it being so quiet outside, car doors closing were as audible like broken glass. She glanced at the time. One twenty-three in the morning. One of the car doors carried the last portion of a party home with them.

"Did you lock the goddamn door? Jesus Christ, lock the door!"

"You need to be quiet," his date hissed.

Then the man started singing, attempting to hit a falsetto that in the frigid air carried like a hyena's dream.

"Darlin', youuu," whomever he was sang, "send me. Darlin', youuu--" Oh, you, hell, it *would* have to be a song she liked. She dropped pad and pen on the floor, reached to flick off the lamp, and drew fat blankets over her head.

When she looked at herself the next morning she made a mental note to soften the wattage around the vanity mirror. A thirty-eight year old woman stared back at her, naked, in a tiny bathroom she'd been naked in, it seemed, every day the rest of her life, barely caramel, enough body to be noticed and a mole on her right breast right where she wished it wasn't; looked like she had a tiny vestigial third nipple. Regina's angular face complemented her mother's wide eyes. Usually her hair was pulled back, fastened with either bow or clip. She was very pretty, actually, in that woman across the hall way, and smiled for the mirror, then pinched the roll of fat around her middle.

What kind of letter really to send Ma? It wasn't enough pretending Dennis was sufficient reason. And what about the other family she needed to contact down there? She was certain she'd seen a postcard in a stack of mail she hadn't bothered with yet, probably more than one, and an invitation, its envelope the brightest gilt-edged ivory she'd ever seen, her name and address in flowing calligraphy written by a hummingbird. Somebody in the Nevills clan was forever getting married.

Stepping into the shower reminded her of Dennis. She massaged her scalp, silently thanking God for good sex.

Stepping out of the shower reminded her she hadn't turned her answering machine on, which in turn made her ponder the vacation time quietly accumulating on her behalf in G, O, and D's office.

She smiled at the image of finding a little island...

While she dressed, after that smile, the spider monkey she had spied accidentally as a little girl danced nervously. The room it skittered about was populated with bric-a-brac women's things like thumb-sized figurines of rosy-cheeked housefraus wearing bonnets as blue as their cerulean eyes and as red as their cheeks, sweeping or cooking, making Regina's mother's cabinets a celebration of pleasant and comfortable domesticity. Sunlight through the kitchen's half-opened blinds fell over Ophelia Nevills in a grid of shadows like a heavy gate. The spider monkey was waiting for an angel to show but none had come. This increased its anxiety. The woman's dead body had sprawled on the kitchen floor over an hour; dead of a heart attack after watching a thief exit her bedroom window, not a clue as to how long he'd been in her house.

(Ophelia herself had been up and about for hours that morning; she was returning from the basement with a dried load of clothing for sorting later, it being Sunday; she hadn't even made the bed; he'd been in her bedroom thieving around an unmade bed.)

Every bodily reaction she couldn't control sprinted off so fast she didn't realize that the heart attack waited in the kitchen, where the knives were, where she ran to, under that heavy grid of sunlight below the cutlery drawer. Her thief had branched into the neighborhood three weeks ago, working out of one of the many vacant houses in the area.

Since it was the last of its kind or more likely the only one it had ever met, the monkey thing had no name; it poked at her body and jumped away. Poked and jumped.

Finally, it lifted her hand and let it drop. Very disappointed and somewhat bored, it left.

When she calmed down from the first few minutes being dead, Ophelia came to realize she was traveling very slowly, or the world's movement was too fast. Ophelia Nevills got up, folded her wash but left each stack on the bed rather than put them in the drawers since that would've seemed foolish, then returned full of vague fears to the kitchen tile to lie again under the sun's shiny gate.

Regina's letter was never sent. After Ophelia was buried, slow rain fell straight down, hitting Regina's upturned face as she searched for lightning, hitting it softly in counterpoint to a desire to hear thunder.

Someone patted her shoulder. Decades of nicotine seeped from his hand. Following the old man's hand brought yellow, wet eyes. Behind those eyes, the longest human thread in her life. He'd even attended her birth, although she didn't know whether or not there was any true blood between them, and had been raised not to be so impolite as to ask. Ophelia hadn't encouraged her to ask questions about either side of the family but had instead, wordlessly, discouraged. Omission was parenthood's most effective tool.

Glancing over her shoulder at Skillet she wondered how far she might trust him, and with her hand atop his she wondered if his ancient touch meant he already knew everything she was about to form the questions to. She didn't pretend she had actually *liked* her mother. Her mind hunted for the right word. What was it, what summed up mother and daughter? Had. They had one another. And now they didn't, and it hurt. What would he say after she mumbled automatically, "I'm OK?" He smelled like hardship distilled but that might have been the rain hitting his wool suit. She tried not to move. She wanted to see his magic work.

She slid her hand across thick wrinkles.

"Finest white woman I ever knew," he whispered for her ears only.

Regina whispered thanks. Her nervous hands sought shelter; they found her pockets. She remembered in one of her mother's correspondences something about death. Ophelia Nevills would sometimes update her on who dies. Everybody dies. "If you return me to the earth," Ophelia had written, "all I can do is grow."

Finest white woman Skillet knew was dead in the ground. In the increasing rain Regina Nevills concentrated on the small flowers around the headstone and the sweet, real taste of the purest word *Mother*.

"Stay her girl," said the old man. He left that advice with her, moving off slowly with the others toward the awning and on toward cars. She couldn't remain at the grave much longer without seeming pathetic. She waited another minute though.

Perhaps, as the living thinned off, she'd glimpse someone off alone by the trees. Maybe through rain she'd see tears in his eyes.

She could chase him, through the mud if necessary, by the neck if necessary, and just look at him. Grab him and yank him around. Then let him go before his attempt to answer. She didn't know her father beyond being told by her aunts that he was tall and dark.

That narrowed it down, didn't it? Tall, dark men orbited her life like poorly-built satellites.

Not bothering to see that there was no one to see off by those dripping trees, she left her mother. Dennis stood a few inches off. Regina's olive eyes met his brown ones a split-second before she went blind with tears. He hugged her. She heard the pastor move toward them but at that instant didn't want him touching her. Everything she'd never liked about growing up flooded her. He was white and he knew God. The rain neither slackened nor intensified; it fell steadily.

"Regina?"

"I'll bring her in, Reverend," Dennis whispered. She listened to Reverend Daville squish across grass that had already been wet from dew. He was almost as old as Skillet, had been a dim part of her life for nearly as long.

Ma had entrusted her soul to this man, her immortal soul, her beliefs and her station in life as lonely Ophelia Nevills. *Why should he be able to hold more of my mother in the palm of his hand than I can show along my entire body?* She wiped her thoughts on the shoulder of Dennis' suit. Dennis led her through the clot of mourners, Ma's acquaintances black and white, and Regina's few close relatives. The aunts were there waiting, Auntie Lisa in front. Regina had asked her thirty-three years ago what color Mama was if she wasn't colored.

Without thinking about it Regina was there. She knew the distinct smell of family.

Lisa's hug produced a swoon of memory. Regina's jaw tightened against her aunt's cheek.

"She died alone," Regina moaned into Lisa's stiff wig.

"No more alone than you, me or Jesus. Pain ain't your friend, girl; let it go." Lisa smelled like home.

Her three other aunts ringed her within a wall of flesh same as they had with Ophelia after their brother disappeared from her life one day.

Regina reached for Dennis and brought him home.

That evening Skillet followed them in his jitney wagon. He felt like he had to. Necessary words, he said he had, and she believed him. They entered Ophelia's house in silence. Dennis quietly watched the two of them before he excused himself.

The fragrant old man sat right beside her on the sofa, too old for preamble. "You miss the one brought you into this." Skillet's voice scratched like coal. "Ain't a secret you hated her most times, loved her sometimes. Ain't nothin' wrong with that. That's how kids do. Today you're probably thinkin' you can't do a thing without her." He stopped speaking and regarded her profile. "You carry yourself like a decent woman."

She didn't even bother reminding him she wasn't a kid anymore. The part of Regina numb from the events of the day broke from reverie long enough to say, "Still died a white woman to you." Race, even in death, was annoying. "She was my mother."

"What d'you believe you gon' die as?"

She absently pinched the back of her left hand and half smiled. "Ma told me it never mattered."

"Not speaking ill but she could afford to say that. Not you. Your mama knew when to listen to me."

Regina watched him closely.

"You saw how most everybody stayed on sides out there, black folks and white folks with Daville floating around," he said.

She remembered the old man's whisper in the foreground of this funeral.

This is your fault, she thought of Skillet. "Been times I wish somebody would call me nigger just to put me in the right frame of mind."

He shook his head. "You don't need pity. You see how old I've got? I done heard that word at least once a day every day of my life."

"You never heard it from Ma."

"No."

"So I'm lucky to get 'Oreo'?"

He shook his head sharply this time. "I'm too old to try to pity you, girl! When it happens you ain't gon' know what to do with yourself. I ain't been old forever. It took me three times as long to live what I got."

She thought of her job. No one forced her to take it. No one forced her to keep it.

"I knew your mama when she was just a girl 'fore most of her folks died out." He shifted to alleviate back pain. "This is when I wanted to be a reporter. What used to be a *newsman*. Long time ago. Thought it would be like sending out letters. But everybody gotta eat, so mama handed me a skillet and taught me. Papa taught me how to do. Wasn't no time for sittin' around thinkin', not like today. Been a long time since you come around. I could see it in your face out there. Something's missing. Pieces of you were gone before your mama died. You got time to think; ain't too late to start questioning what you ought to think on. Opie couldn't give you that since she never thought to learn it herself. You ought to stop believin' you're alone. Ain't nobody heard from you in a long time."

She knew he had talked to her aunts.

"Don't keep yourself weak."

"When did you get beat up 'cause your hair wasn't nappy?" she snapped.

He *hmphed* to sum up his life. "Girl, I been beat down by stuff so small your eyes couldn't see it."

His features were jaundiced and shadowed by the yellow lampshade. He was so aged she hoped one day she too would fall in love with old age.

"When I went to college," she said, "I spent the longest time hoping she'd let me back in her life." A few tears dribbled to a halt.

"She never liked that you left here."

"I didn't even finish college! I wrote letters. She didn't answer. I tried to call, she didn't talk. Guilt was the reason she let me back, not love. She *relented* to being mama."

"Ain't that enough?"

"That ain't enough."

He took her hand and patted it. "Let her rest, baby girl. I know ain't no such thing as forgiving. Wait enough, you'll forget. Here, I won't stay much longer."

"You knew my daddy too."

"Yeah."

"You never said a word about him."

A light went off in a side hallway: Dennis sitting in the dark to listen.

"Now him, we never did understand," said the old man's voice inside Ophelia's house.

"Who's we?"

"Black folk."

"Black folk."

"Folks can't understand themselves, girl. Aunties and me never understood your daddy. Ain't no tellin' where he's at.

Man had too much *something* in him." The light went back on in the side hallway. Skillet gave a little nod that direction. "That skinny black man you got back there, he a good man?"

"He's a good man."

"Then you don't need your father."

"At least his middle name, Skillet."

He adjusted in the seat again, organized a few thoughts, then spelled out life for her: "Your young mama got pregnant down here a long time ago by a black man who left her."

"Were they in love?"

"He loved everybody. Don't mean he bedded around. He was good to people. Had the nickname 'Float'. Whole year before you were born they were as close to married as law allowed. When you came, Ophelia showed up at Lisa's doorstep thinkin' to drop you off. You can credit Lisa for you even having a mama," he said with a short bark of amusement at the memory of that day, Ophelia Nevills scared as could be in that part of the outlying poor neighborhood. All she carried was a cheap cotton rucksack stuffed with baby stuff in one arm, and Regina in the other. No purse. No hat. A rudimentary dress on her back. She tried to show no weakness on Lisa's doorstep. Lisa, though, being familiar with every kind of pain there'd ever been having been born with a too sensitive heart, ushered the woman in and within an hour they were holding each other and crying. Skillet tried to keep himself inconspicuous in the kitchen beneath the sink laying down new pipe. At that time the emotions of women made men uncomfortable.

"I believe she kept the family's last name out of gratitude for Lisa," he said. Gusting winds pushed rain like splashes of gnats against the house, every now and then obscuring the windows with messy spray. It was unseasonably warm, fifty-two degrees outside. Regina wanted to walk out there a while. Back home there'd be snow; she'd need to put on her scarf, her boots, that cumbersome coat. It felt like comfortably-appointed spring here. Kids probably played outside here. Even though she didn't have an umbrella she might've walked out that door.

And only because Skillet was sitting beside her did she decide to move.

Right into her mother's house.

Through the end of winter, through sporadic periods of cloud and light and life in spring, just into the hot beginning of summer, she worked to imbue that modest house with some of what she and Ophelia had kept from it: the memory of a mother and daughter in the front porch paint, the touches of two different generations in the floral choices and style of garden running the length of the fence, the airing of the house when preparing a meal in anticipation of Dennis' visits, treating the once indifferent neighborhood to a sense of hope via the warm aromatherapy of blatant peach cobblers, genuine perfectly seasoned chicken, the impunity of greens, biscuits, ribs and pie cooked simply because the mood struck, the wind creeping in to carry each peaceful scent down the block, so unself-conscious that it would sometimes double back, carrying the scent up a tree or through a backyard simply because it hadn't seen what was there yet. Regina put on fifteen pounds by June first. Dennis flew in whenever possible, about twice a month, and stayed for as long as possible, a day, two days, during a vacation an entire week. Neighbors knew him by his comings and goings, waving his way as he lugged bags from the cab and hopped her porch two steps at a time.

Insurance money, her own savings, and Dennis kept her from having to work till the end of summer. She was able to tend to the house as though she'd built it from the ground up. The basement became her library, set up with sofa, bookcases and phone, to read while doing the wash. The gray concrete floor remained cool down there but rather than carpet she kept a pair of slippers at the top of the landing as well as a plush rug in front of the sofa.

She'd read somewhere that the color blue stimulated creativity. Ophelia had the basement walls painted cream, pink cream. This was changed when the first inklings of the basement as refuge tapped Gina on the shoulder to remind her she hated pink. Too girly.

The basement wasn't large. In a single afternoon she re-painted it sky blue, light enough that it wouldn't absorb all the illumination from the four hanging bulbs. The small sofa fit in nicely opposite the ancient gunmetal furnace with its elephantine trunk leading up into the ceiling. The furnace's fire grate was visible from the sofa. She imagined winters watching its fire, a thick book momentarily forgotten, enjoying the soft heat radiating from the furnace's fat metal belly as she tucked her legs and pulled her robe tighter.

Sometimes in the kitchen, particularly the first two months, she'd pause to watch her mother filling saltshakers, checking to see whether the cabinets needed more whole kernel or cream corn, writing to-do lists, addressing a birthday card to Regina from four months ago. She seemed as substantial at these times as her daughter's own reflection, but ignored the daughter during these pauses, having forgotten that the difference between life and death was the attention one paid to things.

But just because she was usually noticed in the kitchen didn't mean Ma didn't move throughout the whole house. Ophelia intuited that death, meandering, common, bound to visit, was endless in its replaying of life without volition. Ophelia wandered, and wondered if each of her, created second to second of her entire life, was somewhere trapped in an individual locus of time? Rewinded into one-woman plays of each of those moments? She lived for fifty-five years. Were there thirty-one million, five hundred and thirty-five thousand dead Ophelias isolated from her? Perhaps a younger version was at this moment looking for her, one that had known to ask Reverend Daville sensible and proper questions and had thus prepared herself for an afterlife of searching?

She pondered these things without being able to carry them. As such, her thoughts were useless. She was dead.

Victor wrote to Regina only once after she left. His short letter arrived after she'd been settled a month, long enough to contact the few people she felt in some way were left behind. She hoped he would continue his crusade.

Victor, this is my new phone number and address. This is where I'll be, I guess. Didn't get to say bye like I wanted to. Hope this reaches you. My address book got a little wet in the move.

Dear Regina, never knew a person could up and go so fast. I didn't get a chance to sign the card the office sent. I'm sure your Ma's found her pleasant place. Take care. I'll be twenty-four in four months. What's on the horizon?

That night she curled up in the basement, thinking about Dennis, reading a book of poetry from the local library, the house completely quiet; Regina entertained wispy remnants of fear at being the only person in the basement of a quiet house, and smiled at the nostalgia of it.

She read:

Strange and beautiful are the stars tonight.
Stranger still this lovely weather.
Hyacinths in full bloom, the ground a cooling cinder.
I see one who's come to play.
I see one who will fall in love.
One skates the wild frozen sea.
The moon glints aloud; we're so free,
Even me. To glide so fast, spirits we
Be.
And shadows are silver and blue.
Hyacinths breathe.
Leafless trees fan winter's long unbroken breeze.
Silent, then cold without leaves, I sneeze. My soul
In danger of no more soul.
My life in danger of no more life.
This moon in danger of no more time.
Evils swim the frozen lake.
Three evils swim forever beneath me.

She missed Victor. Even missed Atefeh. Life hadn't been life for so long. She started to cry and felt alone. She put the book down and went upstairs to visit awhile with Ma's photo album. Across the street her elderly neighbors, a couple, man and wife married forty years, quietly watched the news.

A car loaded with explosives and nails killed fifteen people looking to go home in the parking lot of a Nashville movie theater. The initial explosion flared the night sky, a brief signpost of tender underbelly rage. Fifteen ghosts now wander that parking lot, looking for cars.

"And I suppose you think I *wait* on you to give me a reason to be pissed? I got. No time. For your stupid. Shit."

Rial answered as best he could. He showed the necessary fear. "You gon' low me for *ten dollars*?"

"Penny," said Buddy-Buddy, who was high and when he was high he was dangerous (Rial Pendle, Penny to anybody who bothered to know him) kept his eyes on the inhuman lump just under the elastic of Buddy's sweats; Penny knew exactly where Buddy strapped his two guns. "I will shootcha bitch ass for a quarter and expect change. I took that money from m'mom's purse, all right? You owe my mama ten dollars."

"BeeBee, you a little buzzed, awright, you buzzed. Come on…"

Buddy-Buddy's hand shot under the elastic of the sweats in search of a lover.

Penny rushed him wildly, aiming a punch straight for the nuts, maybe make the gun go off. Inside the house on the backyard Buddy'd chased him into, a bitterly married couple listened to the violence. Hearts pounding, they dialed emergency dispatch, whispering so that whatever was outside wouldn't find out who called the police.

The shot that went off directly below their bedroom window saw them hurriedly calling again.

When a patrol car pulled up, Buddy-Buddy (who'd bled to death) was very dead and Penny quite gone.

Seeing as the world was overrun with emergencies Penny was well aware of response times. He was a good thirty minutes away, two more blocks to where he'd been heading in the first place, home. He passed Ophelia's house. It shuddered.

Regina went to bed that same night remembering the day of the funeral, remembering Skillet sitting on the sofa, remembering Dennis coming out after he was gone, the two of them falling asleep on the sofa. She thought of the letter from her mother the old man had brought forth; it was the closest reason to the truth for him following her home.

"When did she write this?" She hadn't opened the envelope, but held it in her hands by opposite corners staring at it to deny its sudden existence.

"Doesn't matter. She wanted you to get it when she was gone. Trusted to give it to me," he said with a sudden guffaw, "Old as I am."

"You're immortal." She still hoped to divine her mother's thoughts by staring at the envelope. She didn't blink. Vision fuzzed until she felt the same as she would staring at a large body of water. Inquisitive. Tranquil. Disoriented. She was aware she had told him he was immortal, aware that he capitulated yes, he was; these were distant things, ephemeral and of little importance.

The envelope contained a greeting card.

On the outside of the card: to a sweet daughter; the picture a bouquet of flowers and birds with ribbons. Inside were a writer's words meant to express specific emotions that Regina skipped over—likely universal love—in anticipation of reading those words from Ma's arthritic right hand. She'd never read a final message before. What was it a middle-aged daughter needed to know?

She had a split-second's hope for an outpouring, but a split-second only. Mama had written only two words. Two words followed by the signature, Ophelia.

I'm sorry.
Ophelia.

3

Hyacinth Blooms

Phaedra Justine Mason liked to peer over shoulders.

"Rage," she whispered into the scent of washed hair and roses, "is for the young. You're not young, Ms. Nevills. May I?"

Regina moved aside.

"The lines make them look like fighters. See, if you soften here," she tapped a heavy contour line, "then this shadowing on their faces, just soften," she emphasized, then let Regina transpose words into images, both women staring at the picture through one another's eyes.

"Can you feel the difference?"

She could.

The tone of the drawing had totally altered.

"Avoid outlining," Phaedra Mason whispered, close to Regina's hair again, breathing again because she so enjoyed the scent of roses. "Leave the viewer her part to do."

The sniffing woman moved on. For an introductory drawing course, she expected a lot. Regina already had eraser and conté crayon in hand, prepared to pull her viewer's eyes toward remembrance and joy rather than a hard-edged fracas. She studied the picture. She'd drawn them all jumping for a ball tossed into the air. They clearly had smiles on their faces. Did kids feel rage when smiling?

The instructor, a middle-aged purring woman with the downy face of a peach, moved on to the problem child of the class. Soft, blondish hairs over her entire face, like fur. So pretty. She'd learned not to say anything of use (nothing of a technical nature) to the problem child who generally heard nothing yet always had a response. As far as he was concerned he was already an artist. Had written his first poem and accompanied it with a highly emotive illustration by the age of thirteen. Thirteen was six years ago.

The first day of class, after entering the quiet, sunny room of twelve students perched on stools, Phaedra Mason quick-flashed an eyeball smile at everyone, stood behind her teacher's desk, leaned forward and dryly asked, "How many think this class isn't moving fast enough?"

Everyone got the joke, and everyone knew that the joke would survive without needing to raise their hand.

Except Shaffer.

He raised his hand.

He had laughed, then he heard the symphony of the rest of the class laughing just a little behind the beat.

He sat beside Regina, who now peeked to see what he had drawn.

Pick a memory, was the pop quiz's assignment, *and draw it.*

He had nothing on his page.

The instructor had already said she wasn't grading on realism or technical merit. She could be odd at times. She was, she informed them, grading on honesty.

Shaffer had started and erased so many times it seemed he'd forgotten all about the starting part and intended to accumulate as much erasing as a young man can.

Ms. Mason gave his shoulder a squeeze, leaned in--"Have you ever been in a fight?"--patted the other shoulder and slipped behind him to the next student. Shaffer's puzzled frown instantly lost out to a wash of memories so sudden he had to sit still a moment on his stool in the middle of rising floodwaters.

In the remaining few minutes of the class he sketched out a lily pad, tending to its details the way he used to analyze them on his father's fishing escapes. No wife, no school. Actually, as long as Shaffer never wandered too far, no dad, no kid. They were able to forget, which was sometimes important. He remembered that forgetting had given him fields of lily pads to bomb with rocks, far enough from his father not to disturb the fish.

Dragonflies always did their UFO flying over the brownish water, zigging impossibly away from every rock he lobbed no matter how many handfuls.

He imagined the dragonflies as commanding officers. War was pretty much a given the second folks were born.

And Shaffer also enjoyed the scent of roses! Regina couldn't remember a time she'd gotten so many subtle compliments and reactions to perfume. The vial was mixed to order by a beachside hawker in Jamaica three years ago, a vendor who won her over with the way he smiled whenever she sniffed at a cotton swab and raised her brows. The print of her island dress was his inspiration: little flowers all over it, breastbone to thigh.

"Hey, beautiful lady!" he cajoled using personality as enticement. Personality and a sincere high-wattage smile, a full facial smile, one that promised...

Joy?

"You should smell like a rose! Come here, I got a flower for you." People on the last day of vacations never resist one last purchase. His taut neck kept track of marks who strolled this beach, those who during a week would glance at him, pause, then walk on...

...and on the seventh day he worked, better than any Madison Avenue ingénue's undeserved ego at ninety thousand a year. The fourteen-ounce bottle had cost eight dollars. She let him have ten, and to cap off the deal he watched the contented way her hips headed up the beach into the fat dusk.

After she'd met Dennis and he was forever sniffing, Regina succinctly told him he only stayed with her because she reminded him of the most beautiful thing on earth.

The pre-man next to her, entirely engrossed in his drawing, only noticed his audience after her wispy perfume kept fluttering its dainty wings somewhere in a lush backyard behind the lily pads, brushing against the screened-off patio where he worked against deadline. He looked up as she waved through the screen, her shoulders (a powerful fantasy of a dress on an historical romance novel, man on a horse, woman swept away), her bare shoulders cool and dappled by a huge willow tree. Bare shoulders. He would forever find bare shoulders incredibly erotic. The waving at him was like falling in love with him was like vowing to protect him was like no conceivable reason to recall old fights.

She had pretty eyes; Regina Nevills was staring at *him*, not at his lily pad.

What had he done wrong?

He gave a half-shrug to prompt her.

"You were humming."

"I don't hum."

She smiled.

"You hum when you concentrate," she said. "I've been sitting next to you the past four weeks."

"Never noticed. The humming, I'm sorry, I never noticed the humming." He turned the easel toward her. "What do you think?"

"I like--" He never wanted to hear whether someone liked it or not, only how they felt, otherwise what was the point? "--it, makes me feel like it's spring forever."

"For a rough sketch it's OK isn't it?"

"It's beautiful," she said kindly.

Beauty being the ultimate. He would expect something on the technical merits after that level of praise. Which she did. His lines kneeled before him, and only by bid of hand and hand alone did they rise, level off, darken or crosshatch. He ruled a lily pad, with just a hint of a lake.

A handful of rocks seemed to bound into the frame, high up into the air…

…then plummeted straight through the heart of a green lily pad, tearing holes through the center like paper ripped once then twice again, errant mortar shells hitting the surrounding countryside, rocks falling down like rain.

And then the unspoken truth: in war there *are* no civilians.

He didn't know why but he needed to look away from her, embarrassed by the fleet moment of nothing greater than his eyes caressing hers like the back of a hand brushing against fabric to determine how soft it was.

Maybe if he smiled at her. Older women liked it when he smiled.

"Do you think it's thrown together?" Shaffer asked as the instructor approached again. Phaedra's sparkly eyes caught Regina's and she touched a finger to her lips; Regina acquiesced. Their instructor stood beside the young man. She gave Shaffer's shoulder another warm, matronly squeeze, bending again to his ear.

"I think it's honest," said Phaedra. "Deceit," she said louder, returning to the head of the class. "Technique is deceit. *Function* is deceit. Pencils down." Shaffer's pencil clattered to the floor closer to Regina's tennis shoe than his stool. Because they were obeying reflex at the same time as trying to listen to Phaedra, who had intriguing things to say about function and technique being the antithesis of art, an epiphany in the words for Shaffer, serendipity in the moment for Shaffer, then the painful bump on the head for Shaffer, the wedding of Regina's cousin Lewis turned out even better than anyone realistically hoped. Lewis was a doof, but since Shaffer's wedding portrait exhibited enough of a sense of strength and duty, Lewis was optioned into competing with it, standing a little straighter, paying closer attention to his beloved's three friends than he would ever have to again, leveling off his own need for attention to just below ass strata.

Her gift to Lewis and Diane stood proudly behind the housewares and other marital aids the less imaginative had foisted off department store registers. The effect of the charcoal sketch was like a little explosion that mushroomed out, caught folks up, changed their minds. She gained considerable family points with it, considering how she still lived partly invisible to said family with the exception of her aunts after the funeral.

A distant cousin even danced with her so gracefully they could have been in love. For herself, she spent most of that dance whispering how sorry she was.

Afterward she spent a lot of time winding down from the wedding on the phone with Shaffer's answering machine. She hoped she'd paid him enough for the magnificent job he'd done.

Then the young man started trying to spend a lot more time with her. By then the semester was over and she accepted the harmlessness of an arthouse movie, which, she said, "was the weirdest ninety minutes I've ever experienced in my life." They were headed for her car. Shaffer stayed in a low rent apartment complex a mile off campus, where cars got stolen all the time by a melting pot mixture of families and loners equally tired from running in order to stand still.

"But you got it, didn't you?" he asked. "It was all about what you need out of life."

"I picked up something about what goes out and what's put in. So what do you want?" she asked, ready to be fascinated by youth, but young Shaffer, an innocent really, because of shame that his answer was unprepared he spoke softly, into the wind with the added distraction of having arrived at the car door with her quickly opening it for him (since they'd both had large sodas and no patience afterward for restroom lines). She thought she might have heard him say, "To fly."

She locked her seat belt, wondering why these young men spoke so softly. Wondering why she was such a dirty old woman that they seemed to naturally gravitate toward her. Wondering what Dennis was doing out-state. Shaffer had the kind of wry smile that he loved to turn on. She was well aware he thought he was giving her—and all women similar to her in two respects: older than him and fond of glory days—a particular thrill.

He was a decent young Hispanic with a lock of dark hair constantly in his face. "Are you hungry?" he asked smiling, still ashamed of his timidity.

"No. You?"

"No."

So what chance did he have getting her back to his apartment?

"Would you like to see something?" he asked.

"Surprise me," she said. "With sincerity."

"I don't know that I'm sincere."

She laughed and turned on the car's radio for him. No technique at all!

"I think you are, Shaffer. Tell me what there is to see."

There was a group of kids who would look after cars for people sometimes depending on their mood and the likelihood of being paid. Shaffer led Regina into the apartment structure and nodded a transaction toward the boys, who he knew had watched them the entire time they'd pulled up. Shaffer was good for the money if nothing else.

A mural took up the entire left wall of his bedroom, which wasn't a lot of space; the feat of its creation made it seem that much more impressive. Regina stood just outside his doorway while he proceeded ahead. He introduced her to his mural the way a youthful Jehovah must have presented the earth to a somewhat permissive pantheon, infinitely proud without the taint of *pride* in this manner of seeking approval and worth. Infinitely proud at being able to say, Here, I am God.

The lily pad had been expanded into an entire world complete with a lake. Even the original pad was recognizable, so strangely familiar Regina couldn't help taking a step forward into the panorama, which is what his small bedroom turned the mural into. A panorama. Greens. Blues. Fronds. Concentric ripple circles. A rock, the light switch protruding from it like a belly button, suspended above the water as reminder that silence is precious.

"I got beat up a lot," he said, hoping she'd remember Phaedra's prompt, positive she'd heard.

"I should punch you in the arm now. How long did this take?"

"Three weeks after work. I don't need much sleep."

An argument they'd passed in the parking lot several floors below his window ended with the sound of breaking glass and a curse so vehement both Regina and Shaffer paused to allow it to pass, a few moments out of their lives.

When it was quiet and she could think, Regina asked, "Can you draw me?"

He completely ignored the gunshot. It was just a twenty-two, more of a firecracker than anything else. People were always shooting guns off here. He had no idea at what since there was never any blood or chalk outlines. *Maybe they're just clean*, he thought. "For who?"

"Actually I should probably be going. Don't be so curious." She stood beside him now, surreptitiously assessing the rest of his room and gauging when best to ask the use of his bathroom. His intimacy with himself was apparently dictated by economic means. There wasn't enough space to allow much more than acceptable clutter, the basic bedroom bits necessary for human-status: sweat socks discarded in favor of the slightly dressier ones now on his feet, an easel, a drawing table, cheap positionable lamp, tiny sketches in hand made matte frames, several of frogs…

"I thought you said you wanted to fly?"

…others of birds. All in black and white pencil though, crosshatched or shaded for depth and contour. The wall was the only piece in color. His bed was simple. He slept on it. It was big enough for making basic nineteen-year-old missionary love, but she doubted he allowed the use of his bedroom for that. It seemed to enter Shaffer's world one needed a sacred key for a sacred keyhole. The room was entirely too constrained for love, the tenement building itself, old, weary as it was, desperately looking for love in all the wrong places, was too constricted for love. Throats hurt.

"I wouldn't have done this," he said, leaving inspiration to flutter in the air before her.

She ate this flattery thankfully and immediately wanted him to preserve her, right then, right there, in the nude, she in the nude, not him, just keep going straight on till morning. She'd spoken to but hadn't seen Dennis for a month and during this month, day by day, she'd became increasingly sensual. Shaffer was an artist, capable only of making love within this squalid haven via appreciation, and was so fundamentally rigid that seeing her naked—as long as he held a pencil—would have no lasting consequences whatsoever.

"You smile a lot," he said.

"Could you draw me?"

"You serious?"

"I know you *could*."

"You mean pose here and I finish?"

"Yeah."

"For who?" he inquired again.

He could do it, but he couldn't do it for another man. Not spur of the moment. Not without mental preparation. Not that she'd be naked. Would she be naked? Naked under those clothes? If she was naked, art would mean seeing her through her man's eyes, imagining how his desire might flare right while Shaffer's hand was attempting to find the right curving motion to pin her shoulders to the page; if she wasn't naked, art would mean seeing her through her man's eyes, imagining how his desire might flare right while Shaffer's hand was attempting to find the right curving motion to pin her shoulders to the page, going rigid with fascination, wondrous fascination, marvelous fascination, utter gratitude, that if there was a God...and there likely was...it was genius to have created woman as the very first beautiful thing. The earth and the heavens were good. The secret guitar at the bottom of the ocean so finely tuned to a universe of emotion (its strings which cause the tides which feed the moon under which lies a beach and two lovers who are unsure that life is worth living)—the secret guitar was good. A nice touch. God was good, poetry nice...

But it took woman to provide the baseline by which all beauty is measured.

Regina was about to answer him, hesitated, frowned just as she was about to smile, let the smile come again anyway, and told him the picture was for her but that a friend would likely see it and get one hell of a kick out of it too.

She was smiling way too much. No wonder he thought she wanted a nude.

He told her he could do a portrait in a couple hours, three max to pat it with affection. Plus, he would do it for free.

Free.

Very close to freedom.

When she draped a sheet around her in what would have been a living room had he had a living room—arranging herself on his small sofa—she hoped she did so in a fashion which conveyed something, something essential, something necessary, something for those who would never know her and for her truest self during moments of introspection.

She wanted to show something private. Something more than a hip. What kind of woman would show her nipple off to a nineteen-year-old boy in his small apartment knowing full well men never get over being breast fed? What special qualities must she possess? This is what she wanted to show. She wanted to be more than who she was. She gave an immediate jerk to the sheet so that it fanned out, creating a crooked diagonal grin down her chest and belly. Another bit of shift to expose enough of upper thigh and opposite knee. Men would talk about this for ages. Regina Lisa.

And by anyone's estimation, she was indeed secretly horny.

The breast with the mole thus exposed, she was left to wonder what to think about as distraction while Shaffer heaved and hewed.

Ever since Skillet told her how easy things were, with a nearly visible longing to go back and retrieve all the necessary time to think as he saw fit, she realized an almost mathematical problem with time and subjects, that being most subjects simply weren't worth the time. Dennis had already complained of a decline in the quantity and quality of their recent conversations. Problems with talking were even worse than problems thinking. At least thinking afforded the luxury of easily ignoring oneself.

She replayed the conversation: Dennis with his shirt unbuttoned after a jet-lag nap. She was on a chair hanging new blinds and he sat to watch the dance of her ass. He was barefoot and wore the pair of jeans he'd stored in her house to anchor himself.

"Good morning," she said. The argument had been overnight.

He retaliated, "Morning."

"Conversation, huh? Conversation ain't nothing but hot dogs," she said with a smile, which widened because she knew he couldn't see it.

"Hot dogs." He yawned and stretched like a bear.

"Why's the first thing out your mouth when you see me my poor conversational skills?"

"I'm just saying we didn't say but two words last night."

"And they," she said, facing him to judge his reaction, "were good for me."

"'Don't stop' doesn't count." He got out of the chair and held her hips. She stood on one of her mother's rickety kitchen chairs. Not a single significant new piece of furniture had migrated within these walls yet. "Hot dogs?"

"Filler." She motioned to a rod just out of reach. He handed it to her while keeping a hand on a hip. She had the most perfectly curved hips he had ever seen.

New blinds finally hung, she took a seat in the spot he'd risen from. He, on the other hand, still stood there by the front window.

"Filler?" he said.

"Dennis?"

"Come on, sexy elf, you have to talk to me."

"Dennis, Jesus, most *people* are filler."

"You that lonely up here?" He moved closer. Not close enough to sweep her hair and kiss her, but close enough to move close enough to sweep her hair and kiss her. If need be. He said, "Where'd that come from?"

"Ma."

The best way to deal with this was to not say a word, to appear interested but not overly concerned. It was the way she'd said it. Flatly. As though he could go in the other room and address this with her mother right there and then. Regina would be the third woman he'd been with who had a thing about either seeing or speaking to a dead mother. Women were supposed to have Daddy issues not mother fixations. The world was too confusing.

But quiet loomed too noticeably. "She's resting in peace," Dennis said.

"I haven't missed her."

"With everything in the house it's like she's still here."

"Her things are here. They could be your things. How is it a body can be on your mind everyday without weight? I think, Dennis, you need to be thinking about how easy you have it. You get to fly in, you get love, you get passion, pleasure, affection, companionship, baby, for you I am a many splendored thing and damn if that ain't good conversation, without question and entirely with open arms. I love you, sir. I would think that's all the conversation you need." It didn't surprise her that he was suddenly a bother. He had it too good.

"I didn't mean to start up," he said, palms to the air.

"Well the best laid plans. Button your shirt. You look like you're about to go back to sleep."

"I'm on vacation."

"There's the rub," she said. "More good conversation. Are you writing these down?"

By the time Shaffer finished she still hadn't decided on things to think about. Who to think about offered no fruit either. The mind flitted everywhere. She remembered Shaffer telling her not to move or to move just a little bit, then it felt like she'd gone to sleep with her eyes wide open, brain just buzzing away without telling her anything of importance. There were lots of warm feelings around her thighs and dreams about hot dogs, and subconsciously she was fascinated by Shaffer's self-control. Apparently artistic expression wasn't the flighty free spirit cliché on television and movies. There were times his brow furrowed so much she worried she should get up and soothe him.

"Did you want to dress before you see it?"

She covered her nakedness using the sheet as a toga and went to see how she came out. He'd even thrown in a background. No blue-green cushions on a dime store couch. Regina Lisa lounged on a charcoal-penciled forest floor, a tree stump as armrest with, just behind her, dark woods hinted at and even darker entrances between the trees where little eyes might peer from. He had changed her posture, altered her facial expression. Most times a portrait sketch ended up looking as though the subject posed as fruit. This time the canvas Regina looked every bit the independent being, every bit the twin, but the twin who lived a fantastic life of ordinary things among the trees and little imagined things. She looked like she was thinking of something that only women in forests think about.

Consequences or no, he deserved this quick soft kiss on the cheek. "You didn't change the sheet," she said. The sheet had remained a sheet. No diaphanous gown, no sartorial robe. A sheet to ground her in reality.

He just shrugged, admiring her nearness.

Wanting to judge how he'd viewed her nudity, her eyes instead kept being drawn to the face. She'd hoped for a little attribute-exaggeration, not this incidentalness. That exposed nipple of course was there, but it was just a nipple, incapable of forest thoughts. Her hips and thighs, though, flowed beautifully into and under the sheet. For the first time she could remember she felt physically eloquent. But the nipple? She felt slightly foolish now, not daring. Shaffer had put something in her face that at the time could not possibly have been there. Sorrow. Of a particular kind. Misplaced and wandering.

"Everybody sees me as an elf," she said, remaining at his shoulder a moment more. The musky humidity Shaffer's body etched out quickly prodded her. No point in embarrassing him. Erections were easy as sneezes to nineteen year olds.

"Let me throw some clothes on so I can properly appreciate this."

She sent him behind the shut door of his bedroom. She dressed directly in front of the rough sketch. In class she hadn't the drive to appreciate how well this boy was able to grasp a pencil. Two feet by three feet of a ninety-minute sketch. Biased or not, this was better by a good stretch than the wedding portrait of cousin Lewis and Diane.

Across the hall a woman rattled keys at her apartment door. Regina checked the time. Eleven thirty p.m. She knew by the bulky number of tinkling key chains that it was a woman entering. Rather, attempting to enter. The keys dropped twice before scraping into the lock.

The woman decided to speak when the key was safely in the hole.

"Who that bitch you got in there, Shaffer?"--then a loud laugh at the funniest private joke in the world, held comfortably in that hall like a bag of groceries not to be put down until she was properly locked in and all lights turned on.

When Regina knocked for Shaffer to come out he pretended he hadn't heard a thing, no matter that a fly buzzing in a room down the hall kept him and probably his entire floor awake.

"Landlady?" she asked.

He turned red.

"She have a story?"

"Remember the lady we passed on the way up?"

"That was a woman?"

"According to her, her name means sweetheart in Swahili."

"Really? What's her name?"

He shrugged. "All I ever hear is 'Sweet' or 'How much'."

"Sweet on you?"

"Acts like it. Sometimes."

"Watch yourself. Triangles get ugly. Hate to have to kick your girlfriend's ass." Immediately switching gears, Sweetheart so quickly nulled Sweetheart herself would have trouble remembering her name, Regina gingerly freed the sketch from the easel and propped herself against the sofa. "I can't take this."

Shaffer thrilled at the possibility of her hanging on his wall.

"I can't. It's too good. Not that it's me. But this needs to be painted. She ought to have color in her world."

"What were you thinking about?" he asked, staring into the drawn face, asking it, not Regina.

"I think I was everywhere. Is there such a thing as model's hypnosis?"

"Dunno. You really want me to color it?"

"This much: I'll hazard Sweetheart if you need me to come back for fill-in."

"What about another movie?"

Another movie. He was nineteen-years-old. She was thirty-eight. The dirty doubles. The dirty dirty, much too young (too old) to be flirty—but sometimes life is merrily but a momentary dream, a mood wherein all living things are spectres and whims, and just to prod yourself into living you do something incredibly naïve; you make a decision that's light as an autumn leaf.

The mouth opens of its own accord.

"I'm open to suggestions."

"I'll walk you down to your car."

"Understand though," Regina warned.

"I understand," he said.

"Good," she said, and left it at that.

4

The History of Heat

Ophelia's neighbor, Leanna Hutchfield, once nearly married Skillet. Met him when she was eighteen, he twenty. Leanna was past ready to be married into the world and had proven so by taking up a job at her own initiative, working afternoons at the flower shop, the only one in the colored section of town, that one section of little city blocks and stores and heavy air allowed to black folks.

Webster County, city of Dorset, 19XX.

Every once in a while during this time of war, sunken and wild from having his three bean soup served to him with spit if he got served at all, sunken and wild from shameful fear of correcting some little colorless child's wrong behavior, blood-flushed and wild remembering when he once whipped a white boy's ass, himself eleven, the boy maybe nine, beat him up because he'd happened to hear that freckled face openly shout the word "Niggra!" at a little girl; without thought or volition Web jammed a stick through the spokes of the boy's bicycle, grabbed the boy; said, "If you be seein' one nigga then you be seein' three, 'cause there's my mama, my papa then me;" said it with the venom of an old man in an eleven-year-old body, scaring the living crap out of a boy who thought because he had the speed of a bicycle and there were mostly girls playing that he didn't need the safety of a pack to insulate him from stupidity; put such a fear into the boy that the only reason Web wasn't lynched was the boy swore some other whites had beat him up, big boys he'd never seen before. Every once in a while when he wanted to prevent his teeth from becoming fangs from the grinding, Web "Skillet" Dumas let the flowers and green leaves of Poe's Dry Goods and Flowers draw him into playful conversation with that pretty girl, the one who wasn't so quiet as she liked to pretend. Mister and Wife Poe didn't mind so long as he bought something two out of three times, even if only a single flower that, after the summer weeks stretched, he'd turn right back over to her smiling hands. She knew she liked him enough when one day she just blurted, "What is your real name?"

"You been lookin' after me?"

"Skinny's you are ain't enough to see to be lookin'," Leanna said, fully mature and bold. "What's in your bible?"

"Nobody but you needin' to know me other than Skill." He danced a toothpick in line with his smile. "Web," he told her.

She immediately tried to taste the spelling of it.

"W-E-B-B."

"No B-B. Web. Like a spider."

"W-E-B?"

"Grandmama named me. Spiders are God's watchers. Means I should always have a home."

"You got a home," she told him.

"Grandmama meant anywhere in the world."

"And when you have children?"

"Gate and Shutter," he said straight faced just to make her laughter clear and bright.

"Gate and Shutter," he said. "Figure I move my children up a rung or two."

"I didn't know that was his real name," said Regina. Leanna Hutchfield topped Regina's lemonade off a second time.

"Only real name is the one that gets attached to you. Web Dumas. Boy been Skillet so long birth certificate curled up and died a long time ago." She smiled gums. Pink and healthy. Age hadn't made her decrepit, just made her lose things like teeth and vanity.

A paperboy came up the steps to rap the screen door of Leanna's cool, enclosed porch. Leanna waved him off from where she sat and continued talking, saying first as Regina looked over a shoulder to see who was respectful enough to be dismissed by the slight flicking motion of an old woman's hand, "Boy is the last high school boy I seen deliverin' papers. Most is forty-five years old lookin' like they'd rob you. Charles," she said, leaning toward the opened door of the house loud enough for her husband to differentiate her voice from the gameshow contestants on the show he was watching. "Get the paper money ready. Ernest be back later to collect."

"Yep. All right," issued outward, then came a groan of effort at old bones interrupting allotted rest for yet another few minutes' work.

"He likely has no idea what I said," said Leanna, her eyes smiling at her company. Then she laughed. "Man in there doing twenty different things hopin' to hit the one I asked for, and I wish I could blame it on his age. How's yours?"

"Ma'am?"

"He is the waving-est man! Doesn't he know old folks like to rest their body when they say hello? You know somebody waves at you you got to wave back."

"He's a sweetheart."

"Yes," Leanna Hutchfield agreed noncommittally.

"Yes," Regina said, the exact same intonation, the lilting stretch of that tiny word which usually led to talk about the weather.

"Last time I seen him…look like he was puttin' on a little weight?" The tilt upward that made the statement a question, the tilt that offered the tiniest playful challenge.

Which Regina respectfully declined. "Nooo. I wish."

"Some men lift weights. Some men are skinny runners. Charles fell in love with that cobbler you made for him. I think Skillet come over and got him a little taste too."

"Did they eat it all from you?"

"Baby, it was gone before I could get my teeth!"

She didn't know where Mrs. Hutchfield was getting the breeze that was trying to wedge a cool finger between both women's humid breasts, but she wished to God the dear sweet woman would wrap up a plate and let her take some home. It was hot and her house never seemed to want to catch enough breezes to cool things off without her resorting to fans and air conditioners. Shaffer worked in one of the large home improvement stores, maybe he knew something about putting up porch screens. Regina promised the old woman another cobbler. By August Regina had gained an extra inch layer of Regina, evenly distributed more or less, jeans fit proudly, butt even jiggled if she wore a thin sundress. By September first, the fifth time she'd sat on Leanna Hutchfield's porch, here and now, her elfin face toyed with the idea of crossing the seraphim line, becoming rounder, softer, and even more pleasing to the lips. She strongly believed a man should be able to make love to a woman's face alone, cheeks instead of the sweet breasts, tip of the nose instead of the dip of the navel, closed eyelids for all the deep parts songs are written about.

She'd never thought her entire face very kissable until cooking became both remembrance and a way to pass time.

"He been by to check on you?"

"Skillet?" said Regina. "Not really. Seen him around the store but we don't get a chance to speak." Which wasn't true. Truth was: he didn't speak. Not in the language of a man who knew what her ass looked like when it swung upside down and probably knew exactly how it swung right now. If he couldn't avoid it, then it was "Hello," "Hey now," "Mornin'," Regina-girl," and just once, "Mornin', baby-girl." It tickled her whole morning to hear that immortal old man call her (grown woman playing the part of the hare in the race for middle age) a baby girl.

Later she got to thinking on that. Did it tickle her—and she felt stupid at the dizzying thought—Did a grown woman feel so tickled inside being called baby girl while she pushed a wobbly shopping cart along simply because she had no children but wanted to acknowledge the possibility that maybe unawares she had been thinking of the possibility for some time now?

"I'll have him over that way, then."

Did she want a baby?

"No, I'm OK. Truthfully, sometimes Dennis alone is a little too much."

Charles finally poked up to the doorway, a nod and smile already on the way to Regina, and placed the month's newspaper money on the tray table beside his wife.

"Thank you, baby," she said absently, letting him return to the contestants on *Life's Work*.

"You be out here when he gets back?" Charles Hutchfield asked loudly over his shoulder.

Which meant he had no intention raising up any other time during this day for the paperboy. Or anything else.

"Don't be leavin' that money in plain view," he reminded. With that the house swallowed him up gone. No shuffle shuffle, no additional grumble or mumble. Old people are masters of the disappearing act.

Leanna winked through wrinkles at Regina. "Sometimes he don't know how close he gets to reaching the future early. Like to knock him into next week sometimes."

The breeze picked up suddenly strong, shoving the world along for not moving fast enough. Regina looked at her house across the street and wondered how much of that had made it inside.

"We got rain comin'," Leanna announced.

The youngest children on the block—and there weren't many—pealed with laughter at the sudden gust. Regina could almost feel their hearts. Each child ran into the wind's push, their arms outstretched like ancient fighter jets cocking into position before slinging forward off the deck of some carrier ship. Each little body, at an unspoken apex, suddenly slapped a decisive foot down and turned to run with the wind, arms still out, the added momentum making the very smallest children afraid they might actually start to fly. The wind lulling to normal made them giggle even more.

Leanna groaned at their noise. "Be glad when them heathens are back in school."

"Last weekend of summer vacation. We should be glad they're not teenagers yet."

"Amen."

Nature decided that normalcy wasn't interesting. The wind gusted again, briefly this time, extremely fast, then ebbed to a moderately consistent level.

Leanna patted the seat beside her for Regina to cross over; the girl was probably getting tired sitting with her back to the world.

Leanna would never have made it through so many summers without this porch. Their house was not air-conditioned. Charles had fussed "Why am I going to pay for cold air?" and that he had no intention of freezing himself or his wife to an early grave. Besides, it was comfortable on this shaded and screened porch as long as the screens were kept clean.

A man took that moment to walk by, walked with his usual pinched and nervous stride from years of narcotic stimulation. He was a man who walked like a weak preying mantis with something to hide. Didn't even toss a glance toward the voices on the porch, but left Regina with the impression he'd just seen through that house under Charles and Leanna Hutchfield's name down to its title and soul.

She asked Leanna if she knew him.

"Seen him," said her elder. "Don't know him. Walks around at too many different times of the day to be right. Been 'bout a month since last, though."

Regina continued regarding him. *He's making me want to hurt him* the unbidden thought said. Hurt him hurt him hurt hi—hurt who? She didn't know this man. A soul with its hackles raised was no soul, not one that eased the hold on consciousness in order to feel the narrowing of the eyes and hear the low growl of a thing unnamed. She tracked him all the same though.

Leanna watched Regina watch this man; watched him move out into the street from the path of the pack of giddy kids running the sidewalk in circles. "He somebody you need to know?"

"No," she answered.

She didn't stay much longer, and the question followed her home. Somebody. Was he somebody? Maybe he was. No telling. He had disappeared from sight and mind.

It was still hot. Thick womb heat. She poured a glass of water and sat at the kitchen table. Night again, night by the clock if nothing else. Outside, the sky cotton-candied her immediate world with stretched swirls of burnt umber and thin atmosphere. There were gigantic sunset swaths with occasional stubborn bursts of yellow. In thirty minutes the sky would bruise that arcane summertime purple. Summertime was the only time it was understood that the expression *painted sky* was more warning than poetry, because at night things stirred.

From her vantage through the tic-tac-toe of the kitchen window—the mute blinds that had dropped a gate on her mother taken down for cleaning—night didn't start until the very top edge of the sky, where fire gave way to quieter pastel blues dotted by a single star. A passenger jet blinked across her field of view.

The breeze toyed idly with the curtain fabric. Regina imagined what it must have been doing to Mrs. Hutchfield's.

Sitting at this kitchen table an image of a crazed pit bull brought an easy smile.

Bare feet in the kitchen let her know it was peaceful in this home. Her feet stuck to the floor. Carpeting stored up heat; linoleum, after a while, cooled. Linoleum was such a gaudy word but sometimes it was truly blessed.

Regina smiled again. No lights on in the kitchen. All her surfaces either sienna or gray, the sun not gone long enough to warrant gloom. A breast itched. She scratched it. The only piece of clothing she wore was a pair of green panties.

Sitting at a kitchen table alone is the loneliest thing in the world.

Maybe she should hurt that man.

But for now she needed to go to sleep.

She dreamt about sex. Summertime sex was dicey. Lots of sweat, exertion, endurance iffy (if both were truly in the mood then there was no way it could avoid being truly rutty), but there was Shaffer, thumping into her with the single-minded glee of a freed beast.

And then there was Dennis. Then Victor. Then the man she'd almost married. Then Jonathan Hammer, who blindfolded himself out of shame with the long winter scarf he'd given her ages ago. Then back to Shaffer. Sometimes each man shared a setting, sometimes Regina's parted thighs were the only common locale. She always woke up when Shaffer came his last time, this *teenager* back for seconds, and could never figure out whether she got to come too.

The weekend was over. She stretched and purred like a well-fed cat, then peeled herself from the bed's top sheets, feeling loose and double-jointed. Some recurring dreams speak for themselves.

A shower first, then off to work.

Heading out the door, the neighborhood children bounced off to school. As she locked her door her soul circled once and narrowed its eyes, then dozed through traffic, lulled by the knowledge of the human body as totally insufficient cage.

"This in there, that in here, these stay together, those don't touch." A quick perusal to make sure she hadn't forgotten anything. "Any questions, yell for me."

"Carmen."

"Angie." The foreman held her nametag forward. "Garrett doesn't know how to introduce anybody properly. Angela Carmen Lane," she said.

"I thought it was just me," said Regina.

She shook her head. "Garrett's got this idea he's supervisory so he's supposed to act frazzled and slammed."

"Regina Louise Nevills."

"You ever done this before?"

"Not for a long time."

"We don't officially start for another five minutes. If I'm not around yell for Harper. That's Harper behind the doughnut." She pointed out a corner table supporting coffee carafes, two boxes of fresh doughnuts and a box of bagels soaking air to aid hardening. Harper looked thick as a politician. "If you don't work but two days they need to be Monday and Friday. Harper's daughter works at a bakery. We get their surplus and defects. Haven't found a defect yet. You probably won't need to yell loud for him, he'll be behind that table all day."

Angela waved. Harper saluted both women with his doughnut.

"Plus, for your first few days, I want to pair you up with Dennis, Dennis Sarantonio. He'll be here soon. Already knows about you." She caught Regina eyeing the day's assignment. "It'll be just like riding a bike," she reassured. "Soon as Dennis gets here just hop up and ride."

When Dennis arrived five minutes later Regina was already tickled silly to share the coincidence with him.

They worked for an hour before she said, "My boyfriend's name is Dennis."

"Really?" He leaned to her. "So's mine's."

She locked her door still laughing, tickled at the little things like Harper describing the calisthenics he had to perform to get his daughter initially off her eighteen-year-old butt and get a job; Harper bemoaning the trauma of her pathetic choice of friends; Angela countering that Lily bemoaned her equally pathetic choice of father.

Dennis wistfully looking at a doughnut hole.

She called Leanna Hutchfield.

"How was the first day?"

"I have never wanted to go to work just for the coffee breaks! They're crazy."

"But nice," Leanna surmised.

"They're nice."

"No problems?"

"No, ma'am."

"Charles askin' you got to the cobbler yet?"

"You tell him this one has *your* name on it."

"And everything all right in the house there?"

"Yes, ma'am."

"Good," she proclaimed. "Good night, baby."

"G'night."

She flopped onto her sofa with a big sigh, throwing the cordless phone to the chair across from her. Back to work. She yawned and said to the house "G'night, Ma" even though it was still early.

There was a woman, her same age, had even grown up in this same town although Regina didn't remember her at all,

Reverend Daville's niece, Valerie, who'd become the town's chief probation officer and had never once in thirty-eight years felt the need to up and go.

Two days after moving in, Regina contacted Reverend Daville, not knowing what to say but knowing her mother would've wanted him to hear her voice. Ma would've wanted him to say a prayer and a blessing for her daughter. Ma would've wanted a man of God to keep an only child in his thoughts.

Which he did in the tangible form of Valerie Prine. Day three the phone rang; Regina picked it up; according to him his niece was on her way with dinner and a few essentials the house might be without, and diner beware because he himself had prepared the meal, and if it's all right he'd like Valerie to look in from time to time, until things begin to settle. She's a sweet girl, married to the same man eleven years—isn't it a shame to have to emphasize the same man?—and guaranteed not to be a fuss.

When the doorbell rang she opened the door on a woman pregnant as pregnant could be. She fought the impulse to drop with her palms cupped, and fought a rueful smile, which in turn brought a thin sheen of tears to her eyes. Why would they send such an alive woman to her dead mother's house? So alive. So pregnant that her stomach seemed to proceed ahead of her just to secure the room.

"Oh, my," Regina had muttered, a hand to her mouth.

"Hi." The woman held a foil-covered plate. She was pale and freckly. "The rest of the food's in the car. You don't mind?"

"No, no. If you can find a clearing, sit."

"The passenger door's unlocked."

Regina brought two grocery bags inside. She couldn't believe a holy man had sent this woman two minutes from birth on such an errand. Did the husband at least put the groceries in the car?

"You all right in there?" Regina called, closing the front door with her foot.

"I look huge, don't I? I'm fine. Still a good three weeks before I'm due."

Good?

Almost a clairvoyant, Valerie capitulated, "Well, not so good."

"How many?"

"Just one." She frowned in serious distaste. "I couldn't do twins."

"I mean how many already."

"Oh. First one. Know how men talk about us sleeping with our knees in their backs? This is revenge. Feels like he's nudging my spine on purpose."

"Valerie?"

"Hm?"

"First day *zipped* by. You free tonight?" Regina kicked her shoes off.

"What've you got in mind?"

"Drop some overdue books off at the library. Or had you planned on having sex tonight?"

"Pah! Let me get my shoes on," said Valerie.

They'd done this a few times before. They picked a direction and decided to waste a quarter tank of gas on it, having gotten so much fun out of being lost that it didn't matter that women traveling after dark were not very safe.

"Won't be time to read anymore," Valerie said about Regina's new job. Heat whizzed into the car through the opened vents. She flicked a mosquito off her thigh then slipped a hand under her tank to pop her bra. "God, that's sweet relief."

"I don't know why you even put that thing on."

"Have a baby, get bazooms."

Regina rolled her window down another inch.

"What're you doing? Don't roll it all the way down."

"I'm cracking it."

"It's already cracked."

"It's a long way home for your bazooms."

But worst fears are worst fears. "Wait till we get on the highway," said Valerie.

Jesus, I have never known anybody so afraid of a stoplight, thought Regina, irritated even more by her casual acceptance of someone else's fears when she had plenty of her own to deal with. "Here's a coincidence for you: man I was partnered with today is gay and named Dennis."

"Named Dennis for what?" Valerie intently kept watch on the street corner activity sliding by. "What a minute, how does he even know D—" Oh.

"His name," said Regina, semaphoring with her free hand, "is Dennnn-nnnis. Jesus."

"You shouldn't say that."

"Jesus is family."

"That's not funny either."

"It bothers you thinking it'd bother your uncle."

The car rounded the highway's looping on-ramp. Fun didn't start until they took a new exit at random.

Valerie never rose to the bait of family, the way Regina tended to pepper casual conversation with references to

Valerie's politely crazed uncle, the way she so wanted to goad people into talking about the fact of her mother who died very much white whereas the daughter was still left unmistakably black. No one was willing to play as often as she wanted.

"Michael trying to crawl yet?"

"Can I ask you something?" Valerie said while they were in the vague conversational vicinity of celebrating Regina's new employment. "What does Dennis do?" Clearly meaning the one who sometimes waved to Leanna Hutchfield, town matron. Everybody loved Leanna.

Regina floored it. Huge headlights barreled behind them, throwing both women into relief. Flipping her night shield, Regina muttered, "Fucker wasn't going to let me in."

"Damn truck drivers."

She dropped her speed to fifty-five. "Let him ram me if he wants."

"Stupid speeding in the merge lane to begin with."

"Motherfucker!" shouted Regina. The lights didn't slow. He couldn't have been more than two car lengths behind her. The driver had no intention of matching her drop in speed and was probably thinking about all the cleavage and thighs he'd scoped from his high roost all day. At the first clear opportunity, she leaped her car from his path.

The eighteen-wheeler thundered on, choking them with exhaust, heat, noise and lust, just like a man, over before it started, his red tail lights looking like a bunch of fat, glowing, ladybug buttcheeks.

Valerie caught a glimpse of the driver's elbow and rolled shirtsleeve. Definitely male. Both women's hearts pounded. Valerie felt justified in muttering "fuckbone" herself this time.

"Unwashed dick."

"That's a bit extreme."

"Your point being? To be honest, I have no idea what Dennis does."

"I'm sorry. I misheard you."

"Some people don't give themselves to certain types of conversation."

"Regina, if you don't mind my saying, how can you not know what your own man does for a living?"

When he gives you money, Regina finished, saying, "I've dated enough jobs."

"And it never comes up?"

"I know what he does but I don't know what he does does. Something with numbers. Not when I was paying attention."

"What bullshit. There's too much going on in the world for you not to know."

"Am I bothered?"

"This is vaguely psychological."

Regina shrugged.

They drove quietly a while. The car accelerated and veered toward an exit.

Its driver wondered if she was missing something vital in Dennis' character. Then decided she wasn't.

The area they drove through was dark and unpopulated. Sparsely spread streetlamps only highlighted its level of dark and unpopulated-ness. A huge lot, however, was lit up like an evening baseball game. The cars left there were motionless as puppies too long in a pet store window, whimpering at Regina's car that rolled smoothly by without a backward glance. Securely dug into the ground, fixed by tonnage and tonnage of bone and steel, a factory paid no mind to how the parked cars whimpered for motion. Itself poorly lit, it anthropomorphized itself into an unmindful hippopotamus to Regina's little egret of a car.

She followed the slow curves of the factory's service drive, both women looking out all the windows for things they hadn't seen, signposts to mark this excursion as fun. Regina filled in the various bits for Valerie that led to the finale of her day and ended with telling how she hoped to find time to cook and still maintain a garden.

"And you plan to ask him now?"

"No."

"Why does he get to fly around so much?"

"You probably think he's a drug runner. Black Yakuza!"

"I do not."

So the next time Dennis came out, knowing she had gotten a job but not knowing what she did, he asked Regina, "What d'you do now?"

To which she replied, "Nothing much."

But tonight, two ladies riding around in a small car, for this night the two ladies reversed course, retraced their steps, cruised by a park packed with summer people trying to find alchemical love, mixing loud music and barbecue smoke. They drove through the heart of downtown—nothing new ever to see there—then rode through Valerie's old neighborhood. Evening wound down as evening will; what had been fun gave way to being something to sleep on.

In the midst of powdering herself for bed Valerie handed Michael, her husband, the powder bottle so he could do her back. Standing, she watched the memory of Regina's red tail lights draw away from her, brighten at a corner turn, then watched her red tail lights disappear. It was a memory of brief despair, then it went inside.

Inside, the junior Michael snored softly in a crib beside the bed.

The elder Michael sat up reading the newspaper in his underwear.

He waited until she was showered, naked and ready to be powdered—which was perhaps a prelude, perhaps to sex or at least a good night's sleep with the comfort of his wife—to drape his curiosity across her shoulders in the fashion of a sweet and innocent comment. "Why do you hang out with her?" He sprinkled a liberal dose of powder at the nape of her neck and watched it avalanche down her spine to deposit snowfall on the slight rise of her buttocks. The carpeting in the bedroom was creamy beige so neither cared about spillage which could be walked on and blended in. Spilled powder kept the room fresh so long as it was vacuumed once a month.

He spread the powder into an even coating, although Valerie was so pale there wasn't much difference. If she felt the need to go out he wished she'd at least do it when she might get a little sun.

"Uncle Ben's been friends of her family for years," she answered him. "I shouldn't?"

There was safety in saying, "It's after eleven."

"Mike, I've been home an hour. Anything on the news?"

"Usual."

"Gah! Forgot to take my phone!" She clipped it to the strap of her purse. She kissed her husband on the forehead. "Besides, she and I make hot love like nobody's business. G'night." She kissed her son, too.

Michael shrugged, clicked the reading lamp off, and waited there with his eyes open until Valerie had properly settled.

Robert Michilane, whose neck still sometimes ached, had to sleep too, but it was always a matter of hunting it down. In his dream he and Rial Pendle, a name and face he did not know and would not recognize outside this dream, fluidly exchanged bodies but kept the one consciousness of Robert Michilane.

It was a dream he awakened from immediately to immediately consume something to assure himself and the world that for the moment he was done with dreams.

In this dream he stumbled into a stack of boxes and fell, eyes searching wildly. A boy stopped at the edge of a square to search each face in the crowd. The boy pushed through the square. Where the crowd thinned he saw scattered boxes

Like Robert, the child was sometimes black, sometimes white, but always a child.

Michilane's breath wheezed as he cowered. He had no pepper spray. His legs were weak, his feet hurt, and the pounding, the stabbing, the pain in his head made it absolutely wrong to keep his eyes open. His lips smacked in need of water.

Outside the dream, where folks saw him sprawled on a bus station bench tucked out of their way, Robert sleepily tried to arrange his jacket into a more efficient neck support.

Since the kid couldn't be that far behind, the dream counted ten seconds then pushed out. He ran till he was tired of running then he kept running, until he heard himself screaming again (again), "I'll give you something to cry about!"

Into another crowded square, this one a large field of dirt, clogged with people milling about and greeting or arguing with one another, all ages present, all the same person. It was an Australian with a very thick accent and wild hair.

Robert couldn't stay there. As Rial Pendle his black skin stood out blindingly against the white. The boy would pick him out in an instant. Keep moving, and he might find a place where he would blend for a while.

But he might be seen too.

He might be seen.

Silently, the boy wove through the white men, none of them paying any attention to him. His prey's back was to him.

Three of the Australian selves mutually decided on a fist fight. A wall of disbelieving selves instantly formed. The boy, desparate with anger and cut off from the man, had to shove and weave to reach the place Robert Michilane had last been, colliding once with a wrinkly man who cursed his scrambling back with a passion.

Wild, confusing desires tend to make a man pepper-spray fifteen-year-old girls.

Straight ahead was another alley, thick and shadowed despite the brightness of the high sun.

Robert entered it and crouched.

A few minutes passed.

Then a few more.

Then one more.

For a moment he worried that something had happened to the boy.

Then he heard the footsteps. The boy was coming, slowly and quietly.

Robert jumped him.

But two strong arms and a shoulder slammed Michilane into the wall, snapping his head against unyielding bricks, the arms of Michilanes the boy had recruited to aid in his hunt. When Michilane awoke in the bus station he was seated on a plain wooden bench same grain as the simple trial table to which Rial Pendle regained consciousness if it is true that souls mingle with souls in dreams.

A dim beam of light focused straight down on Michilane.

The assemblage was silent. He glanced side to side. He knew exactly what was going through their minds. It went through his also. *You are no part of me.*

"You are no part of me," the boy accused aloud.

"That's why she left," he continued. Older versions of him appeared pained and vacant.

Rial Pendle stole about outside Regina's house, the bedroom light having caught his eye. The cheap jewelry he'd stolen from the old white lady had barely gotten him high. This new account might fare better. Old lady had probably transported to suburbia the moment she noticed those piddling bracelets missing. Little brown sugar had moved right in, like a second stringer released from the bench.

Robert moved through his years, heading for the children's area, where he found himself as a months old baby. He took the baby from the arms of the teen holding him and returned to the dim beam flung from infinity.

The accusing boy watched the baby's pale chubby arms reaching for the man's scraggly chin.

Too weary to care, Robert sat and rocked the baby, rubbing its belly. Such a tiny person. Beatific. Far cry from being a loser. "Why'd you come?" he whispered. "What's down here you didn't get in Heaven?" Without looking away he spoke to the boy standing before him. "All I will say, after all the living and planning you did, a lot for this man you didn't even know, all I will say is I didn't get here alone."

That was what the dream needed him to know.

A half hour later Robert Michilane woke up feeling like three tons of gold, so huge as to be worthless to a solitary man, so heavy knowledge became tract. Robert gingerly rolled off that bus station bench and knew to refuse to die until he had been someplace truly warm.

The first thing he said to the only person to stray too near him (after a particularly violent coughing fit and accepting a mint in lieu of a lozenge from the man) was: *don't buy into the myths there's a lot of bullshit out there live your life covered in shit nothing but fertilizer, high grade, come time to die.*

5

Ever Wonder What It Is You Really Want Out Of Life?

Teeth finally combed through pubic hair. A rubber penis paused a factory-direct head just inside her. The tip of a tongue parted sections of the hair in order to grease the scalp...and just when she thought it safe to hazard distracting herself by shifting the grip on the clothes line, he pushed the fake member home, listening to the popping noises it made. Her body tightened momentarily. The dildo itself wasn't entirely pleasurable, but the thought that it was *his* hand guiding it, his knuckles brushing, was.

The game, part of it, was that everything be played out in silence, excluding sighs, purrs or sharp intakes of air followed by a delicious good-n-plenty moan. The game, part of it, was for right now she had to hold that cheap stretch of rope, arms wide, legs wide, to see how long she could stand being touched without touching. So far he had circled around her like a slow cyclone, top, bottom, side, diagonal. Nipples. It had started with nipples, the way they peeked whenever she bent. The loose V-neck tee kept falling away. When she stood, nipples poked the thin layer of cotton with hypnotic minds. He simply *had* to pause the world (it seemed paused) while she watched his approach, two steps and he was there, body heat and all, ninety-six degrees and humid outside, head lowering surely for that nipple, teeth closing gently for a second or less on cotton before the other received a thumb.

They completely forgot about the old magazines and the stored clothes for donation. Seemed her Ma had tucked things away in places Regina didn't even know existed within the house, but there was time enough to be good to the world. She was naked, shaped like an "X" for the entire world to see, and *exulted* in it.

Even still, she couldn't help a laugh when he had breathed, "Wait a minute," and after a quick run upstairs returned with a massive pink rubber shlong. She was glad he grinned sheepishly before they began to play.

Now that he moved the dildo out so that his tongue could enter, Regina shuddered pleasurably at the noise of the rubber hitting the floor. Then the tongue left. She trembled. Her arms were tired. As for Dennis, he was trying to keep from ejaculating on the basement floor but every time he touched any part of her his heart wanted to be ripped from his chest and plunged up her vagina so it could explode in a shower of twinkly come. She heard him breathing. Heavily.

Her eyes remained closed.

For a few seconds respite they simply breathed.

A shift in the atmosphere told her he was moving, circling. The hazy envelope of sweat around them altered its shape. He drank her nudity, inhaled her scents, wanted one way or another to consume every sweet, creamed morsel of her from head to soul.

He pulled her close and held her. She heard the leonine purring rising from deep in his throat, gaining until it became a sustained growl. She pushed against him.

Excitement negated the rules. She said two words.

"Eat me."

"Drop."

She lay on a mat. Dennis kissed her. He lapped the sweat at the pool of her neck. He ate her breasts without touching the nipples. He etched her rib cage with his tongue and even probed for belly button joy. Her thighs were already open; his hand went for a swim. He lay opposite the length of her, facing her toes. She kissed the hair on his thigh. She shivered. She played with the base of his penis and she did so slowly, delectably, her lips so warm and wet he imagined he was safe forever. When her lips closed over it the way people eat large cherries Dennis lost all strength and the will to live and slumped his face into her damp crotch, nostrils blowing streams of hot air through a tiny rain forest.

She guided him on his back. If he was going to high dive off a tall gasm, she wanted to be riding that same wind.

She straddled his hips, bent forward to kiss him, and while doing so lowered all the sweet mystery to the tip, to the shaft, to the base of experience. To life.

To the hilt.

Beyond all limits.

Then quiet for five minutes' worth of afterglow.

She wondered what was on his mind.

The floor was comfortably cool to the touch.

Would she ever tell him about her monkey?

He nudged her thigh.

"You glad I bought the dildo?"

"What makes you say that?"

"I felt safe for a moment."

He cooked dinner that evening. And after that, he sat at the kitchen table flipping through a book brought up from basement storage.

In the male and female camps lovers are bussed in. When two warring tribes throw stones at one another, integrate. Two things then happen: some pick their targets selectively and precisely, some stop throwing altogether. Majority, minority, only fashion.

Consider Jack and Prudence. They managed to fashion a love affair out of a few rather tired notions having both grown up during war time and therefore aware of the value of tenderness no matter if it came from God or the Devil.

"You aware this was a library book?" he asked as she flitted by.

"Yes."

"I thought it was about monkeys." He closed it. "Did you want me to take it back next time I'm through the city?"

"What's the difference between psychiatry and psychology?"

"Drugs."

She swept past him, and then by again, doing God knew what.

"That's a weird question."

She shrugged. "Just wondering."

"What are you doing?"

"Putting some of Ma's stuff back." She held out one of the figurines: a bright white chubby woman with red cheeks and a green apron.

"Reverse discrimination," he said, which was enough to make an angel hanging for a moment around Regina warm softly as it followed her room to room and hovered over her shoulder with as much interest as she in whatever knickknack of her mother's she paused to consider, sometimes brushing against her dusty cerebrum to share a memory or two or side-floating an angel it had never met before, one just nosing amongst her things. There were only a few seconds left to this experience before every thought would fade and the angel re-joined beside someone else, something else—frog, beetle, hydrangea, senator—that might finally click into place as the one thing an angel was supposed to remember. Angels glow to show appreciation for brevity.

But in the time it took for such warmth the angel was gone and Dennis had proceeded.

Not enough time, thought the other angel as notation of the other's passage; as preparation for its own.

"I've got the chance to work out here," said Dennis

Regina's back was to him; she lined the thumb-sized ceramic dolls on the high shelf Mama had installed to make sure certain things remained out of a little girl's reach.

"I don't know if I want you living with me," she said, wondering if she should include a blue-haired troll to live with the figurines.

Dennis drummed fingers on the table. "I know. I mean, you probably wouldn't know how to act if I was around every day."

"Yeah."

"Yeah, so, I'll still be around more though, help out with things—"

"Why don't you ask me to marry you?" she said over her shoulder.

He dropped both hands flat on the table, fingers splayed. "You notice how we have these talks your back is to me?"

"I'm sorry."

"What're you so afraid of?" He shook his head at the proposal. "You don't love me enough for marriage."

"*I* don't?"

"I didn't move way out here, Gina. You up and left on the heels of a loss. I've been through enough times of a woman saying well if you cared, and you and me, we're too old to be getting in each other's way that way. I couldn't have said don't move into your mother's house."

"Yet you think I'll let you move in?"

"I'll move when you love me enough to marry me. I was just hoping you might be happy to see me a little more." He motioned her to sit down. "You don't want me to marry you," he said, hoping she detected the hint of a question.

"Are you forever going to wait till I want something before you decide to do it?"

"That wasn't necessary."

"I've told you what's wrong. You're in, you're out," and why tell him she too had felt safe in the basement, too safe to be comfortable upstairs in an easily accessed kitchen where someone might snatch this comfort away at any instant. "I don't want to be a convenience for you."

"How can one person be so selfish? We keep coming back to this. Baby, I don't own my own private jet. Let me remind you who moved. You moved. Me, I'm sitting in your kitchen a thousand miles from home."

"My aunts need me to get married so somebody else can worry about me. Since I haven't met anybody out here—"

"I hope you haven't been looking."

"No."

"That's good."

She wasn't sure if he remembered her aunts. "They want me to marry you."

"Maybe you need to decide your own wants too."

"Maybe," she said, "it'd be nice if you asked me to marry you."

He rested his face on his knuckles. He looked like a confused dog.

"Do you see other women when you're not with me?" Regina said.

"No. Matter of fact two tried. They couldn't get past you and gave up. No, I did not give them encouragement or incentive. I'm just that damn cute." He took her hands; they held in the middle of the table like fortune and teller. "Why I need you," he said. "You steal library books. You smile with your eyes and the tip of your nose. You have the most perfectly curved hips I have ever seen." It was difficult to keep a straight face at this point. "You know—" he bit the corner of his lip to keep from grinning—"how to have fun with a dildo. I love you even though you think I'm a hot dog."

"Never called you a hot dog."

He waited her out.

"Filler. I said most conversation is filler."

"Maybe we should find enough toys where we won't have to talk."

They made love in the kitchen, quickly and uncomfortably but satisfactory nonetheless.

Then they made love in the living room while watching television.

After three or four hours of restful sleep that night she awoke to ask a promise from him, the kind of dream-like promise that in the asker's mind becomes a mission, transcendant and simple. The more she'd dreamed about it the more certain it became that Skillet had accepted such a promise from Leanna Hutchfield, a drop everything (work, family, the safety of common sense) covenant between king and queen, wherein a man recognized that there would indeed always be that one woman who was his queen.

Dennis roused quickly, pushing half-seen dreams aside like dusty junglewebs until he came to the ebony clearing where her voice originated. Into this static-charged jungle a single cricket somewhere outside in the grass by the house tried its best to annoy and interfere.

Her chin rested on his shoulder. The way her breasts pressed against him was marvelous.

"If I die and you still love me find some way to bury me back home. An elephant graveyard. I want," she said, "I want to be the only human anyone knows this has ever been done for. Do it so nobody will dig me up."

She paused a few seconds, her breathing synchronized to his, the cricket creedeeping.

"Bury me with elephants if I die." Not when I die, because death was no more a given than life. She was damn sure Skillet was immortal. "I guess when I'm dead I want to be left alone. I want to be dead and knowing you've done this for me and that the world is leaving me alone. Or the news agencies are sworn to secrecy and they never speak my name. No taxes, no phone calls, nobody looking for me."

"You want to be forgotten in an elephant's graveyard."

She rolled over then because she knew he'd heard every word she said, and she went back to sleep.

"Last night you asked me to bury you with elephants."

This he said while they showered and he soaped her back. She had already played with his erection once so he didn't think anything of it when she didn't answer except to reach back to grab him, squeezing just so a few seconds then twisting for a water-dappled kiss. The poetry of the moment brought Shaffer to mind.

But he was just a boy.

"Remember last night you woke up," Dennis said in the grocery store. She was reaching for mellons. "Those aren't ripe."

She moved to the other side of the bin.

"You asked me to bury you with elephants."

"What were we talking about?" she said frowning.

"We were asleep."

"No, I mean just now."

"Your aunts. Marion—" he said, slightly annoyed.

"Aunt Marion. Remind me to pick up her medicine."

"I took the last aspirin this morning." Headaches, he realized, might become the norm.

Skillet's station wagon pulled into its parking space when they left the store. The day was so hot all his windows were rolled down. It was patient and slow heat, the kind content to cook you up without your knowing until the thermometer popped. It was a fat man sweating and cloying until you needed to snap at everyone capable of love just to cool off.

A blast of noise and tires followed Skillet into the lot from a beat up mongrel car with massive speakers and car doors a different color than the body. A young man slammed his car door, and yelled over the hood, "Man what the *fuck* you doin' on the road you cain't drive with that old ass piece a shit cutting in front of me piece a slow ass motherfucker—"

"Excuse me," said Dennis, there quick to let him know that men don't hesitate. "Are you hurt or you bleeding do I need to take you to a doctor If not back the fuck up off this man show some rightness he did wrong you doin' worse shoutin' out here like you ain't got sense the first or a mama who raised you—" Dennis' skinny body drawn up to its full height, no emotion betrayed anywhere along his body except his eyes which repeated over and over so simply that simplicity became force, *I see you.*

I see you.

I see you, in music too loud vibrating my brain past where it needs to be, bringing the headache back, nowhere to go but up or down, up or down, fool, no such thing as living a linear life if you're born might as well, might as damn well turn around and die, living off manufactured alienation, I got mine real, fool, *I see you,* GROW YOUR SILLY ASS UP, CHILD, turn that noise down and stop driving so damn fast because I see you and you are not enough to be the cause of this.

You are not enough.

You are not enough.

You, oh shit here comes a fist, are not, you are not makin' me chew my cheek, don't make me clench my jaw, turn that FUCKING noise off, ohhhh sonofa bitch!—

"Dennis," said Regina, coming beside him to add the shame of foolishness to this mix, touching the back of her silent old immortal's hand, saying nothing to the man with the reluctant music smashing through his car like a fist after a soft spot, but looking at him. No telling what kind of weapons he had waiting for an excuse inside his rimmed eyes. He smelled of disaffection.

I see you, came from her.

I am crazy. I am so crazy. I am so much crazier than you, came from Dennis.

Of course a crowd gathered. Life was at times as good as TV.

The boy again: "Man, get yo punk ass from me, got shit for you," said Manfred. "Best back the fuck up." He noted for immediate reference the sequoia thickness of the store's

security guard exiting the store. He hoped the woman—
"Check ya man," with a flick of his chin—would accept this
warning and redirect it as directive so he could get the hell
away from whoever the hell this was taking up for this slow
driving no turn signaling old nigga taxi wannabe how the hell
somebody gon' live ninety thousand years and still be po' and
pitiful as shit that I got to get angry to keep me away from
tears somewhere so much of my time?

And Skillet, who knew, who could gauge time like a
weight in the palm of his hand, for the first time turned his
full undivided attention toward the noise coming at him from
over the top of the raggedy car. He immediately knew it
issued from a thing weighed no more than twenty-two years.
He waited long enough for a pause to present itself between
the boy and Gina's man, a pause where his voice, without
needing to be raised, could circle in directly between the two
like the king of the jungle and he said, "I'm sorry." Ophelia
would throw a fit to witness the predicament Dennis had her
daughter in.

Your man got nothin' but eyes, he thought at Regina. *Got
no sense of weight.*

"Look here," he wedged further, "I'ma set it right. Ain't
mean to be in your way."

A bull moose bark came from the security guard.
Everyone turned to see him point a thick finger at the TV.
"Turn that shit down and shop or be out this lot. Gina, you got
your groceries, go on home."

Looking at Skillet, Manfred had the same reaction
Regina did months ago. Will I love myself that old or want to
die? The thought of love alone was cause for revulsion. The
possibility of love for a man already buried six feet under by
wrinkles and dangling skin was fear in and of itself, a walking

skeleton trying to pass atrophied muscles off as living cells, animate, talking to him, *to* him, acknowledging Manfred's life like Death leaving a message on an answering machine. The voice of this old man made him feel like he had no friends.

Unforgivable. The old man deserved to die. They all deserved to die. "Fuck you, nigga!" Manfred shouted. He dropped back into his car and roared out of the lot.

"Boy be dead in two miles," Dennis said.

"There's lessons everywhere," Skillet snipped. "God ain't never let me down. I been on this road forever." No one had noted how Skillet kept one hand in a pocket the entire time. *Boy don't know how close he came over some parkin' lot foolishness.* "Better grab that cart 'fore them groceries go walking," he told Regina. A cart full of groceries. Left there. By both. Ophelia would have a fit. After all the time it took her to learn to accept being thrifty, here was her daughter about to commit the biggest waste of all, inattention.

"You OK?" Regina asked. She moved for the cart. She wanted to heave a brick through the store window. Certain grocery stores had barricades so you couldn't steal its carts. This was one. If the damn store treated its customers like humans she could've wheeled the cart right into that asshole with the loud music! Shopping carts always wouind up by the side of roads somehow. She wedged the cart as far as she could in the narrow opening the restrictive posts permitted, vowing to one night come and steal a shopping cart herself.

Dennis fumed toward Regina's car. He caught the keys she tossed him. What drove that old man to continue to drive this ratty piece of sheer luck in the first place? Jesus, he was sick of people! Dennis was, not Jesus. Jesus was on Mars preparing it for terra forming. People everywhere, gotta drive around them, slow down for them, maneuver between and amongst them, wait for their dumb asses to generate the teeny spark of thought necessary for them to get the hell out of the way, amorphous people who served no purpose but to be constantly in the way! People who had to pick other people up so they honked their horns too long and too loudly weekends when everyone else needed to sleep; people who would never strip naked because there'd be nothing left to see; people who had never seen an angel like he had seen an angel, saw it in the morning superimposed over Regina trying to exactly mimic Regina's physicality while there was sunlight coming through the blinds; people who wouldn't know he had gone to sleep with elephants while hunting a cricket; people who did not share his amazement at being so deeply in love, who didn't want to kiss a special mole or know that he washed her hair and wanted to strangle her because something always seemed to be happening around old people, even this one, who was dangerously close to becoming *people*. People—he thought of what he said through the boy to the boy's mother, and his eyes burned shamefully—who had babies but not children, babies doomed doomed doomed to be pe—

The other jitneys moved in, shaking their heads and laughing.

"She-id! I *wish* he'da done that with me."

"And you wouldn'tna done a *God*damn thing," another one said. Skillet just muttered and shook his head.

"Gon' take time to drive up in this parking lot..." they continued.

"What'd he do, follow you in about five miles, Skill?"

"...and act like somethin' important happened. Done got my pressure up. Ya pressure up?"

"Naw," Skillet said.

"Got my pressure up. All that noise."

"Don't it make you mad? Makes me mad. Probably ain't even legal driving with music up that loud. Windows vibratin' and all. Can't hear no siren or nothin'."

"Fuck, I ain't thinkin' 'bout him," Skillet said, using that word *thinkin'* to effectively negate the possibility of anyone ever remembering Manfred the rest of Manfred's natural life. He left his unlocked car for his seat, the lawn chair he brought with him to put near the entrance or sometimes inside the store so he could reminisce about the death of politics with Paper Don at the lottery counter slash news stand, but usually outside if the day was right enough to appreciate him.

Once her groceries were loaded, Regina interrupted the security guard. Big Chris was impressed by her protectiveness. He fantasized while she told Skillet to watch himself. *Too many fools don't know how to make room*, she said, then tapped the knob of Big Chris' nightstick to get his quick attention. "Watch out for him," she said.

"Like I got time to be watched over," Skillet said. "Girl, go on home. You probably got ice cream in them bags."

"Aunt Lisa tell you I'm barbecuing next weekend?"

"Yes." Then he snorted. "Fool on the road one need watching over. Put his ass back in kindergarten."

"Yes, sir," she agreed. She paused a second to see if he was going to call her Baby Girl just so she'd feel safe, but his hands were shaking. He kept them low and out of view but she saw, so she said goodbye.

Two miles down Dennis asked point blank about the elephants.

"Let's go swimming today."

"Gina!"

"I'll tell you at the beach."

"I don't know how to swim."

"Good Lord."

"Not many swimming pools where I grew up."

It was surprising only because she'd always imagined skinny people to be natural swimmers.

"He shouldn't be driving."

"He drives a circuit of four blocks around that store. Takes the same old ladies to their front doors every week. I used to ride with him. Never since have I been in a car at so constant a speed. Little fool behind him is the one."

"Still best to avoid the avoidable."

A thought struck her. "You ever get buried in sand? Would you let me bury you?"

"Christ Almighty, woman."

"You would." She smiled. "I've never done that."

All I have to do is lie there. Like sex, he thought. And he smiled too.

It didn't take long to get home and change. They arrived early enough to avoid the greater crush. It was a small beach, mostly man made, on the easternmost edge of the city, which presented folks with question marks as to what ocean was out there, at what point did their little burp of beach and water evolve and get away from them, becoming something they hadn't the means or influence to cope with, and could that larger something break off and leave them disconnected from the world? Even the kids swimming here couldn't help thinking of the beach as something that might pop at any instant.

The lifeguard on duty was the same boy who delivered papers around Regina's neighborhood. She wondered if she knew Shaffer. Mrs. Hutchfield had told her he'd graduated his senior year and jumped straight into college.

It wouldn't be noon for another two hours.

Dennis and Regina flew past the lifeguard tower with its peeling white paint and whipped fistfuls of sand at each other's feet with no more restraint than kids in winter. In the movies, the woman arrives at the spot first and drops to her knees, returning wild strands of hair behind her ears. The man falls beside her, exhausted and energized with devotion; he casts about for a reason to touch her long naked legs like a buddy but decides against wasting time; he touches her like a lover, a proprietary snatch and grab of the thigh or knee. Propped on one elbow he looks at her and her alone, a look so full of totality they impulsively kiss before remembering to race to the water's edge to give themselves over. Surf and foam are the whole point of coming; immersion, expulsion, private foreplay inside bathing suit and trunks.

Their bodies exulted in both the heat of the sand and the press of sunshine. The sight of random children building soggy mounds for no particular reason was good.

Regina splashed into the water a split second before he did and—the moment he sliced under—she remembered he couldn't swim. She immediately drew her legs under and reached to grab him, but there he was under the water, legs kicking, arms out in a point, traveling a good ten feet before momentum gave out and he popped to the surface sputtering with a happy laugh.

"I thought you couldn't swim."

"Not on top. Not too long on bottom."

His makeshift trunks had that sudden vacuum-packed look that always made her laugh at men. She looked him up and down then kissed him lightly. "Walk with me," she said, and took his hand. Sand squished between their toes. The water resisted but didn't really try to stop them. Hand in hand they walked straight ahead, all the way to the outer netting, their bodies bobbing like the colorful buoys ringing the net, toes stretched downward to keep in contact with the sand. Water slapped them in the neck and face.

Dennis took his hand from hers the moment the water level tried to trip him up. He held his arms out for balance. He turned around. The distance tracked away. This was a *lot* bigger than a bathtub. This water was real. It knew he was in it.

But Regina was shorter than him and breathing fine.

"We walking back now?" he hoped.

"Actually, we're going to swim back."

"The deuce you say!"

"We went three quarters of the way holding hands. You won't drown. You've never let me down; I won't let you either. It's not that deep."

He set fear aside to be fascinated a moment, appreciating the horizon of sand underscoring city from a vantage he didn't normally see. "Never been this far out in water before."

"This is where we need to be."

"You like swimming?"

"I love swimming."

"How come I didn't know that?"

They hadn't given their bodies time to acclimate to the water. He was trying to keep his teeth from chattering. She moved to him, chest to chest.

"Feel that?"

She'd managed to peel her top down without him knowing.

"Feel that?"

She'd managed to worm her hand into his trunks.

He almost lost his footing.

"Grab the net," she said, issuing random tugs.

"Don't make me come," he said nervously, imagining his come floating through this water for the next five years greeting tourists as local color.

"I wonder how long I can hold my breath?"

"Come on. Gina. Lifeguard."

"If he's observant he might learn something."

She tightened her grip.

His eyes flew open.

"You're going to get us put out," he said.

"All he sees is the back of my head."

"He knows we're out here."

"I've always found that swimming makes my nipples hard."

Like an idiot he agreed, "It does," feeling their small points jabbing at his beady chest hairs. Her hand slowed its ministrations, and the warm water spliced with cool currents felt like paradise.

"You either swim or come," she warned. "It's your fault for wearing shorts and not having a pair of swimming trunks. I couldn't get my hand all in here otherwise."

"No?"

"I'm pretty sure."

"He knows what you're doing."

"Does he have his binoculars yet?"

"No."

"Let's see how long I can hold my breath."

When she came up for air, just before his eyes prepared to roll back, she coughed and sputtered water out her nose, so sexy in his eyes a halo surrounded her.

"That's not easy," she said, stifling another cough and pulling hair aside. Four seconds. Not enough to pop but more than sufficient incentive to make him see things her way. She made sure her top was firmly in place then pushed backwards to float.

"They're going to kick us off this beach," said Dennis moving toward her.

"Lean forward and follow me in," she said.

"Forward?"

"Like this." She twisted to stretch herself upon the water. "Keep your feet behind your hips and your body angled like Superman."

"Like flying."

"You're my Superman. Keep your momentum forward and you won't go under."

"I'm still hard."

She smiled and pushed off.

Leaving the water, they sat on the sand at the surf line and watched the sky for a while.

"I know somebody who could draw you," Regina said sometime later on the beach. "You're a very handsome man."

"Thank you."

"You comfortable?"

"Considering. Ha! I feel like a hot dog!" Sand covered him neck to toe in a billion grained sarcophagus. "I think I'm starting to cook under here."

"I love you."

"Feel lucky enough to marry me?" he asked.

"Actually, I do."

"I believe everybody has seen at least one thing they weren't supposed to," she said.

"Saw my father naked," said Dennis. Drops of water trapped in his kinky hair sparkled.

Absently, she sifted sand through her fingers, leaving a layer across the toes of his feet. A man had asked her to *marry* him. That shouldn't have felt strange but it did. She had never really felt a part of anything and now she was being asked to become part of another human being.

She continued laying sand across his feet.

This was extremely scary.

But wasn't that what IT was all about?

A whirl of questions swirled about her head. How could a woman who had never truly felt important in her life convince a man of sincerity? And she desperately wanted him to know she was sincere about everything she said and did. The elephant burial sounded crazy but it made sense. It really did. Quests used to be a regular part of everyday life. To search for, deliver to, keep from, aspire to, congress with. Used to be but had faded away for no good reason. The world, being all about connections and revealing and seeing, was something to get away from for a while. Privacy was necessary, and death was about the only private moment left.

Had she really agreed to marry him? Five minutes of burying his toes hadn't led any closer to coherence. Explaining to herself why it was good to be married while explaining to him about the potency of summer nights and the ineffable loneliness the sound of a cricket could prod loose didn't seem to help, but he understood it was a loneliness which permeated even death. Most people in coffins cry uncontrollably. Regina visited her mother often enough to know that cemeteries, no matter what time of day, never escaped the enforced quietude of night.

She told him about visiting her mother. The wind, spring wind, slightly chilled, blew. It disturbed the grass around the headstone with the sweet word *Mother*, and even at ten in the morning it felt like night.

In the summer bees flitted dangerously close, leaving the living with a greater sense of living, and sweat annoyed the spine. If the wind blew in the cemetery it did so like an ex-friend. The wind tended to be ignored. Other mourners, off with their own dead, tended to be ignored. There were never many anyway. As folks stared down at their graves, as folks dredged up loss, the world tended to flatten out, become slate gray above and behind, funneling background noise into their ears without assigning distinction to any particular sound except cars: car horns, car doors, the susurration of traffic sometimes; the knowledge that someone had arrived, someone was leaving, there was point A and while one stood immobile the world was not prevented from reaching point B. Life went on in cars.

Graveyards were terribly, terribly lonely places, and the earth itself was a huge, indistinct graveyard.

No more.

She had agreed to marry him. He needed something to solidify himself. "Will you let him draw you?" she asked, knowing asking Shaffer might be awkward but he'd relent; there was no choice. Shaffer was an artist, and the world was losing subjects in droves.

"I'll think about it."

Sometimes Dennis was unsure what to make of things. Things like poetry. And certain stories. Poetic stories. Things that didn't hopefully explain themselves or go where they were supposed to go. Were the things he didn't immediately (or ever) understand a benefit in a way he didn't actually need to understand?

In addition to seeing his father naked he'd also seen a woman who inhabited three distinct bodies. He used to wait during lunch for her to pass his spot in the park to see which body she had that day. He knew her by her walk; over a three month period he fell in love with her body language because it was his secret way of knowing.

He sat at Regina's kitchen table. He was surrounded by a house that was all the house of Regina and Ophelia, not of James. "My last name is James," he murmured. The kitchen counter was not the color he would've chosen. He hadn't carried that refrigerator in; its weight was outside his experience. He didn't like blinds, he liked curtains.

"My last name is James." He wanted to marry this woman! Had wanted to marry that other, mysterious woman. She might have loved him if she'd known he was the only man alive who knew what she was. He should've approached her. Passing, she had to have noticed him enough times. He could've said Hi. But she was beautiful each time, and it's impolite to talk to a woman simply because she's beautiful. No metaphors. *She* was beautiful. She wasn't all women. He wasn't particularly shy. For a while he'd become obsessed with getting there on time to see her pass, to see how she pretended to be *people*. She dressed like a secretary. The park was littered with secretaries and pigeons, some off by themselves, others pecking together in cross-legged groups around the rim of the fountain he liked, the one of Athena with its halting water supply regurgitated from cruddy bronze fishes into a pool that practically cried because no one ever looked into it. It was silly to feel sorry for a Goddess in downtown Briar.

I needed you, he imagined she thought of him, *to love me too.* The accusation shrunk the Nevills' kitchen around his heart. She was the ghost whispering forlorn admonitions. "I could've loved you," he defended, lost. You should've implored me to believe.

Swimming in belief the way Regina asked him to believe.

Regina who asked him to bury her with elephants in Africa. A thirty-eight year old black woman from Dorset, her thoughts and moods melted down during the night to a fine tip of gold, gold simple and pure enough to be edible without spectacle. Eaten like a cracker. Buried with elephants and betrothed on the same day.

He stole in to watch her sleep. Weather stayed too hot down here, a factor he hoped wouldn't affect him too much. She slept so wild. Sometime tomorrow they'd talk some more, try to understand the functions of love. He rested against the doorway, arms folded, naked, suddenly wanting to wake her and admit, "I can't sleep." *Your sketch bothers me.* He saw eyes in the woods behind her, beady red ones that chewed the knucklebones.

He grinned at the word.

Knucklebones.

The mind's eye saw her breast on paper. It excited him. That meant it excited the artist. "Pervert," Dennis whispered.

What else was in this house besides him and her? Naked and bored, he explored.

He touched things he had never touched before. Original paneling. The servile figurines in the kitchen. He'd never held them and looked at them the way he looked at them now in the light of the refrigerator. He went to the basement and walked around without turning on the lights, feeling like a ghost, afraid to find himself already waiting down there.

He made it to the small sofa, the center of it, and spread his arms out. He studied the dark, letting the basement's forms coalesce into images until he stopped trying to ignore his body's nervous signs. Ever so slightly his stomach tugged at his groin. He took a deep, quiet breath and brought his vulnerable arms to the cushions, pushing himself to his feet.

The basement followed him upstairs, a yawning maw thrown over the interior of the home so quickly he could do nothing except head straight and single-mindedly for the bed to clunk in beside Regina, who might wake up or at least unconsciously snuggle closer to him.

She kept sleeping, snoring softly.

He decided that was enough.

6
Part 2
"together"

Gideon's Bible

The wedding occurred months later.

The moment Dennis kissed her Regina let go the last of the ambivalence toward Reverend Daville's officiating. She never bothered to realize before how every wedding was a self-contained fairy tale. With one kiss: over. All planning, all expectations, life up till then, all over. The groom's as well but the line was, "You may now kiss the bride." The man was released out of the starting block a split-second before her.

Not that she cared. Her aunts, front row behind her, masked disappointment that she hadn't chosen their church by beaming rapt attention at every word the Reverend said, burning the ceremony of their brother's daughter's marriage into memory for the historical retelling of it.

Dennis covered her lips like a warm blanket.

Everyone wanted to eat.

She had to force Shaffer to put the video camera down during the reception.

"I think you look very beautiful," he said.

She wanted to tell him, *Shaffer, I don't have a clue what I'm doing,* but instead gave him a hug. "Get something to eat."

It seemed every second someone she didn't know or recall inviting was pulling her away with advice or pride.

Angela Carmen caught her during a moment of particular exasperation.

"You must not've been to very many weddings," she observed.

"Why?" Regina bobbed up and down in search of Dennis for the cake cutting.

"Because you think you're supposed to get to sit down."

"You ever marry?"

"For a minute. Would you like to get on my shoulders?"

"Where's Dennis?"

"Harper's got him."

"What's the two things most people have till the day they die?" Harper was saying, then answered himself. "Bills and kids. Very little difference."

"Time to cut the cake, baby."

"On my way. Pleasure meeting everybody."

"He thinks he's done with us," said Dennis Sarantonio, to which Angela Carmen nodded agreement.

"Before you kick my new husband's ass we need to cut the cake. Bye, big brother." She kissed him, Dennis, on the cheek and pulled Dennis along.

Away from the group Dennis whispered, "Harper was the gay one?"

"Yep."

Finally the time for opening gifts rolled around. Regina's smile, strained and over-used, was at the point of snapping and taking someone's eye out. She hadn't spent five minutes in the presence of most of these people in her life. "Small weddings are myths," Valerie told her during their initial planning session. "Invite ten people, twenty-five show up. Probably some kind of cosmic balance."

Valerie jumped in to do the reading of the offerings. "When the maid of honor stands, everyone please shut up." The reveling leveled.

Shaffer slid by, getting a tight shot of her.

"I need the best man. Mr. Dumas."

Skillet, suited and aftershaved, rose to her side.

"Tryin' to hurt yourself getting to a pretty woman, Web!" hooted Leanna. Charles, who'd given Regina away, shushed her.

"I planned to put both bride and groom on the spot and have them make a speech, but since they look very, very willing to do me harm, Mr. Dumas and I would like everybody to stand, join hands, and offer a moment of longevity for these two, then would the family remain standing for a round of applause for the work that went into the whirlwind planning and execution of this beautiful affair. Without much love left to the world any time two people decide to snag a bit more a celebration is well deserved. I don't know everybody here but we all know why we're here, and I think that's reason enough to offer my own thanks for the honor of seeing Regina Nevills, my friend Regina Nevills, marry a wonderful man who from here on out can happily gain weight. And then we'll open the presents." She stepped back. Skillet stepped up.

"I want to say…" He spoke with pauses. "…this little girl here scares me. She's up here getting married. I can't think of her as young anymore, which means I ain't young anymore. Mr. Dennis James, I wouldn't have stood next to you if your manhood wasn't decent. This woman who took you in is weaved in me. Weaved so through my life you cradle a good piece of me whenever you look at her. I hate to tell you such a thing before your honeymoon. Regina. Regina is going to keep you happy same as you been keeping her. Everybody in this hall done had at least one skinny joke. Matter of fact, ya'll need to just write 'em in the book on the way out. But I'ma agree with this young lady here." He took Valerie's hand and brought her forward. "The weight you're about to put on can keep your feet planted, head from swiveling here and there, peaceful mind focused on one thing: Ophelia's girl. Your mama—"

"Bless her," said Aunt Jean.

"—is proud of you, Gina."

They paused for applause, prayer, and more applause.

"Lisa, Jo, Baby Jean, ya'll get up here help us open these pretty boxes. Where's Marion? So short I couldn't see you. Ya'll want to keep getting clapped at, get on up here." Applause followed the aunts to the bridal table. "Now get to openin' like you done found something on sale."

"Are there any omens about getting married on the edge of winter?" she asked somewhere between the first and second times they made love that night.

"It's not even November."

"In four days."

"Beware of snowed-in newlyweds."

"They don't get snow often here but when they do it's memorable. Sex or aggravation do us in?"

"Likely both."

Then there was the morning Dennis recognized the back of the employee's head. What was his name? He'd done the wedding video. Two weeks of marriage made Dennis forgetful.

Shaffer!

"Shaffer?"

The young man turned.

"I don't know if you remember me."

"Fifteen close ups of your face, I hope so."

"Didn't know you worked here."

"Won't catch me wearing a bright green shirt otherwise. Need..?"

"Windows. Don't have a clue but want some good storms in before the cold sets."

"I can show you where they are. I don't know much about them installation-wise."

"You think the two of us could figure it? If you're interested. Gina told me you helped with the porch screens."

"How soon?"

"Whenever. I can wait on help. I was hoping the store had an installation policy."

Shaffer bloomed a grin. "Windows your idea or Regina's?" Regina probably had this man whipped already. Served him right.

"Mine. Bad as the slice of summer was, I expect winter to be worse."

"Somebody told you about our weird weather."

"What can you do about weather?"

"Weather is as weather does."

"Yeah."

"Lotta heat this summer."

"Bad winter?" asked Dennis.

"Gets that way."

Shaffer got home that day embarrassed at his loud green shirt. He tossed it aside and slid into his lake, lobbing a shoe at the light-switch-in-the-middle-of-the-rock to end another long day.

Around midnight he sketched in the outer room.

For over an hour Sweetheart's apartment across the hall had been strangely quiet. The love song station she usually listened to had suddenly stopped wedging past his headphones..

And she remained quiet. Off schedule.

Shaffer dropped the charcoal, dropped the pad on the sofa, put the headphones in his pocket, and stepped to Sweetheart's door.

A sliver of light underlined it.

Then the door opened on him.

"Shaft, what in fuck you doin'?" Sweetheart moved aside, propping her machete in place by the door. "When I have enough to afford a good gun I'm going to shoot your ass through the door."

He watched her walk away, bony shoulder blades, body half naked in a lacy slip. He watched her slender buttcheeks shifting just enough to cause an involuntary flush at his groin.

"What you still up for?" she asked.

He locked her door. "You expected somebody?"

She shrugged. "Felt the floor creaking. You standing out there peepin' my door."

He continued watching. The slip was thin and here she was, in front of him, a man. "You don't give a good damn, do you?"

"Fuck you, Shaffer. Come help me move this."

"What?"

She entered her bedroom. "My bed. I'm tired of sleeping by the window."

He followed her where she had already moved a broken dresser and knick knack crates aside to swing the bed out.

Her bed was bigger than his.

"Slide it sideways," she said. She bent to heft one end of the mattress. For a scrawny woman she had nice breasts. Seduction? She'd never form the thought much less waste energy on the attempt.

"Doesn't it bother you I don't react?"

"Huh? Shaft, if you want these tits get down and suck 'em so we can get this bed moved."

"I'm saying you need to cover up sometimes."

"For my daddy I'd cover up. As I ain't got time to worry about you, I don't. Got your grip?"

"Ready."

Mattress, box spring, and frame were moved. One mystery was solved. Sweetheart had spilled a glass of water on her stereo.

"Ain't moved so fast to unplug something my whole life." Love songs were her lifeline.

Shaffer never saw books. Sometimes there was a women's magazine, usually when there was some handsome black actor on the cover being celebrated for having a black girlfriend or wife for more than two months.

Sweetheart told him about some actor—Shaffer didn't recall who—who swore up and down he didn't care what color a woman was as long as she had that certain look in her eyes, which must've been blue since the only women to drape his arm had tawny white breasts.

"See, it's motherfuckers like that—"

At the time he had to cut in. "Sweetheart. It ain't like you had a chance."

"Boy, fuck you."

Her TV was on with the sound muted. What did she do inside silence?

Shaffer stood lump-like while she replaced her bed covers.

Perhaps she was thinking about the night they discussed the actor because she sat on the edge of the bed, smoothed the slip over her knees, and frowned the question, "Would you like me if I was somebody else?"

"If you didn't say fuck me all the time?"

"Fuck you."

"What about me?"

"You can draw. You never ask for nothin'. Maybe if I was to walk around like high yellow you had?"

The only woman he'd ever had in his apartment was Regina.

"You act like a virgin sometimes," she said.

"I could fuck you blind. Did I say that out loud?"

Sweetheart's laugh was loud, and grated like *madre's* constant puttering used to whenever she was upset at Shaffer's father. "Fuck you again. I ain't about to walk around like high yellow. I'm sayin' is that the kind of woman you need? Old enough to be your mama?"

"What about you?"

"Twenty-six."

He was tactful enough not to show surprise.

"What you doin' at my door?"

"Don't know."

"You need to know, late as it is. Probably got somethin' to do with that woman. Look like you get haunted." She started giggling. "With her mature wisdom and loveliness and the smell of spring in her pussy."

"Be careful."

"Stupid ass like yourself probably don't know the difference between pussy and the smell of tuna, let alone spring." Her infectious giggling fit caught him up, an evil, delicious giggle. For a hot moment they both laughed pointedly at one another, him sneaking peeks at her body while she made sure those peeks didn't come too far apart.

"Know what? You gotta stay with me all night 'cause you're locked out your apartment like a sitcom."

"Men don't get sucked off in sitcoms."

"You're not nice."

"I got my key." He patted his pocket.

Unspeakably, she patted it too. She broke the utmost unspoken rule. She was sick of rules, especially considering how carelessness with water had forced silence on her. It had been too quiet for too long, and this boy was two feet from her pussy efficiently moistening itself. She was glad she'd showered. If he wanted the smell of spring he'd better get it tonight before seasons changed.

The floppy shirt he wore hid the erection that jumped the moment she touched him. An image, her hair in a simple flattering style, the blemishes on her face lessened with medication, maybe the stretch marks on her tits smoothed with cocoa butter and an extra inch of skin added overall by a good diet, also a few books, not a lot, not Shakespeare, not Morrison or Morningstar (maybe Marquez), nothing necessarily demanding or impossible, just a little something that required hunks of peace snatched like sweetbread to the starving, and some music which didn't rely on "Baby, please" or "Oh Baby, please" sung a hundred different ways, a bit of conversation about something neither knew much about but in which both were willing to make leaps of sturdy logic, a bit of interesting ignorance; an image of her with her real name in subtitles, him teaching her some Spanish, her teaching him, what? Swahili? He doubted very much her given name meant "Sweetheart" in Swahili, doubted with the same certainty that his father spent very much time fondly recalling their fishing trips as anything more than opportunities to get away from his demanding Hispanic wife. It took Shaffer the longest time to realize his mother was demanding not because she was Hispanic but because his very anglo father was lazy. Shaffer, who was probably the only Hispanic in the world with the first name Shaffer, middle name Martin, last name Brolen, very much doubted an image like this had any place affronting Sweetheart in her own apartment in the middle of the night, while she sat beside him warm, flushed, slightly fragrant and very unmindful of how her nipples played against the fabric of her slip. She had very pretty shoulders, smooth, rounded, not bony at all. It was disconcerting to travel through arousal, confrontation, shame, aversion and guilt while simultaneously trying to maintain nonchalance.

She looked him dead in the eye. Her hand remained on his thigh.

"Show me your dick, Shaffer."

"I don't think so."

"Just show me. Shit, you came over here for something. I got pussy, you got dick, and I got a half hour before I like to be asleep. I don't even care if you think about your high yellow bitch that I can't help but notice don't come around here no more. I'm thinkin' you're probably backed up a bit and can't draw with sticky hands. Don't know who you be fuckin' outside your apartment but I do know you ain't done much indoor sporting. When I fuck I fuck 'cause the itch hits, you know? It's just like going to McDonald's. Don't want it all the time but every once in a while mama wants a Big Mac. I don't bring men up here 'cause I more likely than not have to cut the motherfucker. Life's too short for that kind of drama." She gave a low wail, commanding, "Mother*fuck*, give me your hand." She snatched the one nearest well beyond where rules had reason to go, quickly concealing it under her slip. "I ain't permed, moussed or gelled so forgive the bush, but that there—" she curved his fingers inward—"is where you make love to a woman. Put your finger in more." She wiggled her legs wider.

Shaffer jerked his hand away and bolted upright.

"Oh, shit, oh, shit, oh, shit..."

"What's wrong—"

"Shut up!"

"You know how long it took me to realize I got no time for bullshit?"

Sweetheart's pussy was on his fingers! "Oh, shit..." *It probably won't wash off.*

"Get your ass on home, Shaffer, I'll get you some other time."

He was pacing and muttering. "I'd need a cast-iron condom to fuck you."

Which she heard and ignored since seeing him finally riled and human made her smile.

"You can unlock the door anytime you want and go home, Shaft, I ain't in love with you."

Fucking less than real, he thought. "You are less," he said. "You want to be less."

"And whose pussy you got on your fingers?"

He moved for the door.

He unlocked it.

"When you comin' back, Shaffer?"

He quietly closed the door behind him.

Somehow, somewhere, there's a Charlie Brown special titled "It's the Little Things That Kill You, Charlie Brown."

The hot dog and sausage odor kept up its daily assault on Robert's stomach but he had arrived at a quick truce with his Beefdog Pushcart job. It was out of the weather: the sun, the rain and the quick winds. In a few minutes his kid would be coming by. Three months and he still wanted to call the kid Tony.

He spied Tony approaching. The one thing he did not like about this job was summed in the word *customer*. Not the ones who stopped at his cart but the ones who came to buy something for their homes, bought it, and left. The constant sliding open and closed of the doors. Absolutely sucked but annoyances were the only way to pass the time. Men would sometimes come in with attractive wives. Men got their asses kicked; women were seduced. Took a second. Kids who didn't enter orderly were swiftly disciplined. People with infants were ignored, since they'd already entered into a greater punishment on their own.

The kid was trying to turn him into an artist, telling him to study faces as customers entered. Imagine them in the mind not as reproductions but true creation. Take what is seen in one quick moment (facial expression, choice of clothing, hunch of shoulders, flip of hair, weight they'd allowed themselves to gain) and distill it into a raining vapor the hand forms into shape. Here's a sketchpad.

It had some of Shaffer's pictures in it, three unfinished alien things, eerie almost the way pieces of people were snatched out of their lives.

Hadn't, though, to this day been a Michilane born with drawing ability worth a rat's damn. He tried. Kept the sketchpad with him every day, even sometimes intently belayed boredom with it, scribbling out without shame misshapen heads and chaotic figures.

Robert handed Shaffer his usual gratis lunch of sausage, chips and pop.

"Helping a customer this weekend. Figured I need some help myself," said Shaffer.

"Don't you need somebody that works in the store?"

"Man, they don't work *in* the store. Know anything about storm windows?"

"I do."

"It's a little extra money if you're not offended."

Michilane had procured this job because who cares who stands behind a hot dog cart? Hitler on parole could be handling your next kosher dog as far as Beefdog Pushcart management concerned itself. Vendors never grossed enough worth the trouble of stealing anyway. Robert Michilane was crumpled to the point of forgetting whether life held anything worth taking offense. And since folks don't usually apologize for offending he usually wasn't aware of it.

"Money is money. Still don't know where in fuck I am in this city but I'll get a map."

Shaffer chomped his sausage. "Lower your voice. You OK with grunt work? It's only a little money," he stressed. "Didn't seem like the guy knew his butt from a gun turret," said Shaffer; The old guy tended to communicate on the level of battlefields and non-sequiturs.

The vendor remembered to wipe his hands on his smock after scratching at his beard. "I'm in." Beefdog had strict rules about tong handling. Having read Sinclair Lewis' *The Jungle*, Michilane had no idea why.

Where mysteries come from:

Preface: "George Sumner, poet and naturalist, majored in anthropology at Peck University, Baltimore, for fifteen years before realizing he had no aptitude for structured study. The books *Sumner's Guide to Primates* and *Buck Wild*, both likely to remain obscure, are available through Erilax Press for as long as his publisher's beneficence holds. Mr. Sumner currently has plans for one more book, a concise psychology of theology.

"Mr. Sumner will be ninety in five years and lives with his daughters in a perfectly idyllic setting he wishes undisclosed."

There is a species of ape with near prescient abilities, I'm sure of it. The elders of Juala--by elder the average age being one hundred and two--sang songs of their childhoods during a series of ceremonies closed to all save myself and the eldest elder's eldest son, whose job as a minor was to unhurriedly sharpen thick plant shoots and drive them into a circle around the group's perimeter. Several of these songs implicitly or explicitly contain mention of a half-man who enters children's dreams to satisfy an insatiable curiosity. (To avoid contamination of the griot only the elders are allowed to speak English.)

As best they could translate, one of the old songs went:

Juala? Juala sleeps the long hand fly
Juala! One eye open, the long tail mine
Juala? You don't sleep
Close the long hand's eyes
He might fly
And if he flies away
He comes back next night.

Another was an extended tale of the "man-before," so lonely it plucked off all its hair in order to watch each strand regrow. Finally, when men appeared in Juala, the man-before was able to walk the world. Except by then it was in the firm habit of plucking. During the day, hairless, it walked but no one noticed. Juala, it seemed to the man-before, had gone blind. Lonely, it took to roaming during the night; a time when no one was supposed to notice it and not noticing wouldn't be so hurtful. At night its hair quickly returned; every morning it was plucked again.

One sunny day a girl, eyes downcast after being scolded, spotted the man-before's shadow as it hesitantly coalesced. The girl saw this from the corner of her eye. Peripheral vision has since been esteemed in Juala.

Not wanting to disturb the image, the girl observed without moving her head. When she spoke she did so in the same fashion, without moving her head. Sensing the heavy weariness of the shadow, she addressed it as Father, the custom of Juala from a child to a man it didn't understand. "Father, why did it take so long for you to appear?"

The shadow scratched its head.

The shadow sat on the ground.

Eventually it wrote in the dirt, "I wait for men to grow more hair." Seeing that the girl did not know more than Juala knew, did not know that the scratches in the dirt were words, the man-before's shadow spoke. The words fell in the girl's hair where they should have stuck. "I wait for men to grow more hair."

The elders playfully hint that the man-before's text, the first words ever written in the dirt of the world, solidified over time into stone and exist as they will always exist, somewhere deep in Juala, where the jungle does no one any good so no one misses or even knows enough to think about them.

There's a phrase in Juala: 'Bu-shan Jos.' Heavy O. Means "after light."

The elders laughed when I called the man-before "Bojangles". But at home, while my notes came together and my thoughts sought connections, a title became increasingly comfortable to me with its maudlin romanticism. I smile fondly.

This connection feels quite right. I call the man-before "Mr. Bojangles," to give him a face, that half-glimpse of someone one could've sworn one saw before. "Mr. Bojangles," to provide my own primitive artistry to over a thousand years worth of mystery and joy.

Where mysteries go:

The most surprising thing about Ophelia's storm windows (the house wouldn't truly be called anything but her mother's) was how much fun it was getting them up. Seven windows in all, six ground level, one attic.

The scruffy guy Shaffer had brought along was wicked with a dirty joke:

"Rich guy at a bar tries everything to get the kind of woman make your buttcheeks lock accept a drink from him. He's begging, he's pleading, wants to show her exactly how much he can buy. Finally she goes, 'Give me five thousand dollars I'll let you french me.' OK. Gives her five thousand. Frenches her. Still won't leave her alone, so she says, 'Give me your car keys, I'll let you squeeze my ass when nobody's looking.' She stands up, nobody's looking, he squeezes her ass, gives up the keys. 'How about a little pussy?'"

"This isn't going to end with a cat, is it?"

"Shut up. She says no. He plops his bank card on the bar, writes his pin number on a napkin. 'Tell you what,' he says, 'I trust you. Take this, withdraw as much as you want if you promise to come back before closing time and give me a little hit of pussy.' She thinks about it. Guy's too damn persistent. Finally says OK."

He hushed a moment because Regina poked her head out the door again. Dennis and Shaffer pretended they didn't notice her.

One hefted. The other toted.

Her head retracted.

"So she walks out. Titties. Ass. Guy's dick so hard it's crystalline. An hour passes. Two. Bar's emptying out. Bartender's like, 'Hey, rich ass, get the hell out of here.' Rich guy begs and whines. 'Might as well cut my dick off I don't get her.' Bartender assures him there's no way she's giving up, so Richie's desperate. Says, 'Make a bet. I don't get that pussy you can cut off my dick.'"

"Old bartender looks at the lemon slicer.

"''All right,' he says.

"Closing time. Everybody's gone. Richie's about to give up when in walks dream girl, new leather outfit, titties popping out, jewelry up the butt, sweetheart is wet head to toe in his money. Guy's looking at her like shit I'm broke but this *will* be worth it. She walks over to him, tight leather skirt barely covering that ass.

"Richie grins, catbird seat. 'Where's my pussy?' he says like he owns shares in it.

"'You want me to give it to you here?'

"'*Please* give it to me here.'

"Comes up to him, pulls her skirt up to her hips, puts her face close to his, opens her mouth...and blows."

Regina poked her head out again to make sure nobody had fallen off the roof or something after their raucous laughter. Except for the presence of the weird guy, her house became a truly embraceable home with men working on it. Shaffer (Regina went back inside where the nippy wind wouldn't bug her; pieces of a vacuum cleaner were situated on newspapers spread on the floor; two screwdrivers had rolled under a heap of greasy paper towels), Shaffer had suggested a winter garden, and kept Dennis busy in a way Regina had never had a chance to see before.

Two more repair jobs for this vacuum. After that, a respectful burial. Using the long tweezers she reached inside its casing and pulled out another fat dustball, having never been able to permanently seal the hairline crack which allowed dust into the inner workings to begin with. Then a few bursts of compressed air and she was ready to reassemble just like in her college days.

She hummed while she did so and didn't notice her mother entering the room, who noted the mess with disinterest without noticing who caused it at all. She sat to watch the television, which Regina had not turned on but which captured Ophelia all the same. *Life's Work* was on. She tuned in like all of North America minus Canada to see who might be winning sums of money she would never realistically see in her life. God was present in game shows. Did she remember to get her usual lottery ticket, Regina's birth month and day, eight twenty-seven? She must have. Every other day she played it. She remembered thinking, the day her baby was born, she had the right to be happier in the future than any other mother. This tiny caramel baby was entitlement.

After a diatribe from her daddy on why exactly blacks were not to be loved—this was the morning she got put out—Ophelia retorted, "There's no telling how much black you got in you, Daddy!"

The front porch sat disbelievingly stunned. Sarah, Mama, Edric, Aunt Tee and Daddy.

"Is this my house?" he pointed out, sounding like a cocky old politician with just a slight loss of memory. Didn't raise his voice. Questioning expression on his face. He turned to see who said nothing. His wife said nothing. Nobody else planned to say anything.

Well, dammit, let me jog their be-damned memories. "Is this my goddamned house?" he snapped, waiting for some answer from this pack of sudden idiots he'd forever have to carry around his neck so the world could identify him as the one with the nigger daughter and the useless family. "Gina, at least would you please, is this my house?"

"It is. Honey, it is."

"Sarah, get whatever your sister needs and pack it up. My duffel bag's folded in the chest."

"Daddy, I'm not leaving."

"Get me some money out the kitty," he told Sarah, who had no difficulty moving toward the door. Her and Daddy had about as much nigger in them as Robert E. Lee. Ophelia had graduated high school already; Sarah hadn't. If Ophelia had no shame for herself or family then she needed to be gone.

"Girl, I love you," Daddy said during Sarah's absence, "but you got ugly in you. Not me and your mama. Through and through other," said Daddy in one flat, level tone. "Come in the house, girl."

He fixed his wife with a glance. "Keep out here and ya'll best stay hushed." He entered the house.

Ophelia shot glances at her mother and aunt before following. As soon as Sarah heard them enter she dropped the duffel by the door and resumed her station on the porch.

The kitchen, being the furthest from the porch, was where Ophelia's father stopped, poured two glasses of water, and turned to face her. Her slack arms contrasted with the legs that she knew vibrated the pleats of her skirt. Her nose ran, eyes welled, throat burned and she prayed to Him Everlasting not to break down and cry like she was a minute from doing.

"Drink your water. You lay with him? You pregnant? I ain't got time to soften butter. Many boys I done had to chase from around you and you settle on a nigger?"

"He was in the army, Daddy."

He slammed his palm on the counter. "Drink your water!" then called without looking out the back door, "Skillet! You 'bout done?"

"Yes, sir."

"Daddy, you're gonna hurt him," she stated in the smallest voice she'd ever heard.

"I ain't thinkin' about your nigger. I know a nigger lay with anything opens for him. But not with you. No, ma'am. Your mama tried to lay with one once and I like to beat the blood from her. Cut this knuckle open on her tooth," he said, pointing the scar out. "Not since have I laid hands on anybody and not since for any reason will I. Your mama killed that much love in me. At least she had the grace of being sloppy drunk. Has she ever taken another drink since? No. Comes down to my first child though, come down to you, to lecture me about loving them. I don't hate a nigger; I got no *time* for them, see? Skillet can come fix up but when he goes home I don't need to think about him. If you don't remember another day in your life remember this one because you made a decision today opening your mouth to me like that in broad daylight. I think I tolerate enough with this family. I will be damned if I'm going to tolerate my own children." He rubbed his palm then took a swallow of water. "You gone."

"Where am I going to go, Daddy?" She was openly crying.

"You gone. And you remember this day properly. I ain't done a thing but stepped out your way."

This was the part of *Life's Work,* the nation's favorite live broadcast game show, where they interviewed the contestants. Quincy was a bricklayer who one day hoped to sculpt incredible art. Sheila, the podiatrist, whose husband's love in the audience grew with each correct answer—he would never leave her, wouldn't think of it—Sheila hoped to use whatever her winnings to help fund the latest Loch Ness expedition (but told the host that she wanted to travel with her husband and son to several outlying monastic areas of Japan; her son's love of everything exotic, coupled with his remarkable fluency, for a sixteen year old, in both spoken and written Japanese, was simply too infectious to ignore). Reggie needed something quietly bigger than what he currently owned, like a sunken tub or marble inlays, with enough left over to buy up the vacant lots which bracketed his home, erect a privacy fence, some sound baffling, essentially create an island without piers before a neighborhood showing sure signs of decline sank beneath the waves to join Atlantis—except he'd certainly move first.

The fourth and last contestant, an elderly lady of Somali descent with sharp eyes and a penchant for surreptitiously praising God (praise stopped by the host during a break; religion and top rated game shows didn't mix. Your host, Ron Chiamp, had learned that lesson well long ago having muttered "God damn" into a live mike during a similar break in taping on the short-lived *Have I No Shame*. Martyring himself over a diseased wife was the only thing saved his career)—this elderly lady, actually only eight years older than Ophelia, and like at least one contestant on each and every show, aspired only to quit her job (she didn't take to the concept of retirement), say see ya to family, and travel.

Life's Work, far from mere escapism, was all about *escape*. Its viewers were the loneliest people in the world. Its participants were the neighbors of those loneliest people in the world, neighbors frantically climbing fences and scrambling to run, all behind cheery smiles and insincere banter with Ron Chiamp, the loneliest of them all.

Ophelia never missed this show.

This particular episode had aired February twenty-second, nineteen ninety-one, a Friday, the day Ophelia had begun to suspect that the long rude cold she nursed might have progressed to bronchitis.

She coughed. A raspy, human, bad muffler hack, shocking in the way it suddenly did away with silence, all violent phlegm and panic. Coughed and coughed and reached for her tea, some obscure herbal of Skillet's urging, right in the middle of the part on *Life's Work* where the contestants were asked to sum up their lives. Coughed so hard her eyes welled up. Coughed until Regina looked up from tightening screws, frowned and went back to tightening screws. Regina rose stiffly, turned the vacuum cleaner on--which rattled loudly and full of spite for having been disemboweled again by this woman who took care of it out of frugality, not because she cared. It quieted. She was satisfied at her layman's handiwork. She did a quick bit of vacuuming around the perimeter of the newspapers, then left. Ophelia remained with the TV.

Regina wanted to see what all the laughing was outside.

Mysteries are fodder for humor.

"Woman's ahead of a guy, she's got a wedgie from here to Idaho. Joe Chivalry figures he's doing her a favor; pulls it out. Lady turns around and punches him in the eye. Later, his friend sees him with *two* black eyes. 'What happened?' 'First was for pulling a lady's wedgie out.' 'And the second?' 'I put it back.'"

Shaffer groaned. Plumbing was paged for the second time. He tried to remember if he was plumbing today.

"You ever kill anybody?" Robert inquired.

In stride, in stride. "No. You?"

"No. Think I'm gonna get a tiny fan to blow this hot dog breath away from me. How old you again?"

"Twenty this December."

"You got wheels within wheels for that lady," Robert noted, recalling the pretty smile she flashed Shaffer thanking him for the great help. "You're too fresh to Chihuahua a married woman."

"Let me explain once and for all what I feel for this woman." *This* woman, because she was a presence. "In some parts of the galaxy there are stars that burn solely because they have planets around them. The circle widens, a Stonehenge that breathes: she of the Earth, she of the Heat, she of the Little Wing; now add in the darkness as is proper, as is right. Where blows the wind, for the wind was the soul? Or something. If only one person in these tales of tragedy gets out alive—and nobody gets out alive, Robert, each ending is tragic—that one should be me so I can continue to work on another portrait till I start to cry and laugh and split apart at the soul from the secret of not wanting to possess someone."

"What's the secret?"

"Love doesn't come from wanting. Comes from needing. Everybody wants to fall in love, Robert. People that want to fall in love shouldn't. They should wait till they need to."

"Till they need to."

"Yes."

"So you don't want her."

Shaffer wondered if the shudder that went through his body was visible.

"I need to know that at least one person in my life deserves remembrance. That's all."

But Robert thought Shaffer considered himself already old and wizened too much of the time.

"Right now she's one of those people," added Shaffer.

"That's very noble. You don't want her?"

"No."

"So black guy's out of town, her toaster breaks down?"

"Look, I know at my age sex is the end all and be all of experience unless I grow into some real emotions, but I need inspiration at this time in my life even more than I need my mother, seeing as I live in a shithole—"

"What's gonna take you out of there? Stop watching game shows."

"What do you know about getting anywhere, *viajo*?" Shaffer said grinning. "She read my mind," he shared, eyes going out of focus recalling that day when she and he had thrown, joyously, forcefully, with soft eight-year-old fingers, their handful of rocks into a sweet arc, fascinated at the destruction such a simple act could cause; sharing a synchronicity of thought, an empathetic vibration, feeling eight year old guilty elation since in war there are no civilians and, God, with the right machine in hand it is positively *godly* to kill, except really—and everybody knows, everybody does—killing is never godly.

"Ever have those moments? Like out of the blue or from deep in the black? Click. Good, solid click with somebody before the wheel turns out of sync?"

"My wife used to say I changed channels too fast to see what was on."

"We at war, Robert?"

"Always."

"Tell me another joke so I can go back to work."

7

Interim

"What was her mother like?" asked Dennis.

"Your grandmother raised you," Lisa ventured. She nodded at his hands. "The way you snap them peas," she said.

"She helped."

"You know, Ophelia made it a point to hate little things. Broke her heart to find out she was named after a woman driven crazy by love."

"Regina said her ma was always trying to push culture at her."

"Here's what's funny: she knew Othello, I had to be the one told her about Hamlet. Ophelia wasn't that common a name. I thought she'd find it interesting. She used to bring library books to Gina's daddy and me." Lovely the way peas plopped into the water as indication of how good they were. Mollifying how quietly accepting they were as they sank beneath the water at peace with God's plan in a poetic and agnostic sense. "Girl *absolutely* hated her name. Get these tiny looks on her face. After awhile I got tired so I started calling her Lee. Didn't like that either. White folks, no matter how they pretend, got everybody beat hands down when it comes to being crazy. I think most times they're like an accident got everybody stuck in traffic and all we can do is sit back and cuss at the wreckage. Weird was she would rather been called Opie than Lee. At least 'Lee' didn't make you sound like a cut-rate baby doll." Lisa leaned forward with an indecisive frown for a better look at his pot. "You think that's enough?"

"Nobody ever had too many snap beans, ma'am."

"Ha! Son, keep breaking." She yawned and stretched, looking way too sexy wearing jeans and a plaid hunting sweater. Hellacious hips seemed to run in the Nevills clan. While Dennis mulled on the overwhelming likelihood that as little as ten years ago if their paths had crossed he'd have looked over his shoulder (if no one else was on the street; he was, after all, a gentleman) to get an appreciation of the rear guard of her forward motion, and also wondered if Gina's father was a tall hippy man, Lisa (who for sixty-two looked maybe fifty) searched for her remote and turned on the television. Neighboring states had received a freak blanket of snow, and Dorset was expected to get a taste of the same. She mainly wanted to know how bad the weather might get in order to badger Skillet to stay off the road, stay off the streets, and eat soup in his house. *Old people,* she thought. Worse than two-year olds. The second she became old her sisters were sworn to keep her away from the secret revenges in which the elderly sometimes engage.

"...produced record lows in the plains states. As this mass travels east we should expect to be brushed by the tail end here in the lower portion of the state, with an amazing four to six inches of snow spread over the next five days." The map changed. "The good news is that, for the immediate weekend, while it won't be Wonderful William Weekend Weather (William Pounast, three years junior college, one year internship with WDMB, divorced and bitter but photogenic enough to parlay vengeance into wildly inaccurate forecasts), it will be much milder than what's coming and unfortunately what will likely stick around through Thanksgiving and the weeks beyond, the result of a gigantic arctic mass settling over the States."

"Sometimes," Lisa said with the ninety-eight percent of her attention not needed to listen to William Pounast but while still looking at his multi-colored weather maps and computer graphic cloud swirls, "a good pre-holiday cook up does right by everybody. Give me string beans, greens, stuffed thigh with a touch of wine and a little more of that wine on the side—"

"You like white?"

"I love white. You like red?"

"I love red."

"Know what's best?"

"Grape," both answered.

"Nothing," said Lisa, "is better than the juice that's fresh. I know you know about cooking windows?"

"I can sit to this day and look at a cooking window all day and feel nothing but joy."

"And don't let it be gloomy outside."

"Paradise."

"I have found a good chilly October to be the best time for cooking." She tried picking up her pot but a sharp pain in her left wrist told her otherwise. "Help me get this. Move it to the kitchen." She checked on the pies. Two sweet potato, cooling, two lemon meringue, baking, one fruit jubilee, two slices curiously absent.

Windows fog up throughout the whole house when pots, pans and ovens work overtime to bring either order to the world or a spicy touch of chaos to too much routine. In the presence of these cooking windows children sometimes stop to read. They sit in living rooms without turning on lights against the outside gloom and listen to conversations of life coming from the kitchen. Regina, being tall for an eight year old, was allowed to help reach for things. It felt as though the warmth and brightness, even the aromas in the kitchen, came from the single naked bulb over everybody's head, particularly since there were few other lights illuminating the cramped house. Gina saw and giggled at how Aunt Lisa intentionally bumped Ma with her hips to make her dance to the side where Aunt Marion was already standing.

"What you gigglin' about?" chided Marion.

"Nothing."

"OK." Which translated. "Squeeze around your Ma and get me another pat of butter."

"Lee, any your folks get sent to the war?" asked Lisa.

"Ain't happy unless you're prying," Marion said.

"Jesus'll help me when he gets around to it."

"Ma, what folks you got?" Gina asked precociously.

"Mind grown talk," Ophelia said.

"Yes, ma'am." She handed the butter to her aunt, becoming that child-like variety of invisible again.

"Somebody needs to explain to me like I'm five years old why we're forever at war," Lisa went on.

Marion shooed the invisible Regina out of the kitchen to wash up and get dressed in the good clothes laid out for her, warning her not to get them dirty before they left.

"I bet there'll come a day women will war instead of men," Lisa went on.

"Only reason we don't yet is men want us around to supply more boys," said Ophelia.

"You get—" Marion tasted the spoon of sweet potato mash Lisa held to her lips—"the feeling men don't like men much. Bit of cinnamon."

"I guess I should go change, too," said Ophelia. She wasn't entirely comfortable going to a mourning party with them but had promised she'd be there.

"Everything here's just about ready," Lisa said.

"Don't cry," reminded Marion, meaning when they got to Mr. Reese's house. "That'd be inhospitable."

"I don't plan to cry," Ophelia said.

"You cry about everything," said Marion. The only folk Ophelia had from war was their brother Grimm.

"Call your wild child in here," Lisa said as Ophelia left. "I can't melt the marshmallows over these till she's had a sample too," which is what Regina waited to hear, reappearing instantly for absolute, sheer pleasure. Little mouth open like a bird's, smiling her tastebuds onto the spoon. This was important. Sweet potatoes creamed, sugar, cinnamon and butter added turned the potato cream into something else, something that cleared the mind, stirred the soul, and offered thanks to God.

Until the *Age of Realization*, that is, when it smacked her in the forehead (it was her mother who smacked; punishment for a flip mouth en route to someone's grief) that this food, glorious and sweetly edible, was not cause for celebration but was always trotted out like a bus running on time to those people who laughed too loudly in lieu of crying, station to station, home to home, children in one room, adults in another, and they were allowed to play, that's what confused her all those years: kids in their good clothes running around freely so long as no adult was disturbed directly and things were left in their place, and noise levels never grew that any one adult couldn't hear what another adult said; what child, no matter how well-dressed, wouldn't sometimes miss a cue to heel? She knew she had to heel on a dime but that hadn't bothered her notions of joy one bit. Up till then she liked the knowledge that she'd tasted a spoon or fork or tear of all this food before it was carried and set out on someone else's parlor table.

The Age of Realization didn't destroy Paradise, it turned it into a melancholy paradise. Cooking windows became solace, quiet time for the absorption of strength; *an intake of fog*, she started to think after hearing grown folks at a mourning party declaim how lively it once was to listen to the radio, when to get anything approaching an experience a body actually had to *listen*. They talked about mysterious times, particularly those of a man able to cloud people's minds, *The Shadow*, who wrapped himself with the strength of fog. "Intake of fog," from a poem in a book her mother kept hidden.

She breathes and feels my hand's secret sighs
To fill her with dreams, this intake of fog.

She was thirteen. Wasn't hard to figure out that particular take. Breathing deep of the steam. Inhaling the sweet nothings of life. Consuming the vapors. All kinds of flowery expressions she'd pieced together from Mama's cache of hidden books. *Bosoms, bodices, breasts!* She loved her mother's world and couldn't wait to be old enough to join in, steamed up windows, hidden books and all.

"Call up your wife and tell her don't forget," Aunt Lisa told Dennis. "Ms. Miller does *not* like the potatoes diced too big in her potato salad."

"That would be blind Ms. Miller who ought to have food big as can be on her plate?" said Regina.

"Gotta dice 'em again, don't you?" Dennis said.

"Yes."

"I'm not in this. Bye."

It was also about this time every evening that Jesus Johnson made his way home. He was sixty-six and walked with a clipped stride. He carried a cane he didn't need except to sometimes shake while shouting, "No other way! No other way you gonna see God! No other way! Not through me but through the son. No—"

His voice, burned out years ago, struck as a cute rasp, pointed but not hysterical, and directed at no one except everyone. Jesus Johnson spent the greater portion of each day reciting this message downtown. During the bus ride home he was quiet; people on buses had no time for the gospel.

Plus only nuts couldn't keep their mouths shut long enough for a bus ride home.

"No other way you gonna see God!"

Dennis peered out Lisa's curtains as he passed.

"Is he alone?"

"Got a dog. A lot of books."

"Doesn't carry a bible."

"I think he memorized it before it was in paperback. Won't utter a single verse out loud, though."

"...no other way," the scratchy voice trailed.

Lisa's curtain dropped into place.

"He's been doing that maybe three years. Hasn't stopped since."

"Nobody knows why?"

"Not when a man shouts with conviction. Even the first time wasn't a shock. Matter of fact," she recalled, "I was gardening. Heard him coming, looked up, saw it was Mr. Johnson, listened to him for a minute till I caught the whole cycle, knew he wasn't sick, and went back to gardening. Everybody on the block's old anyway. If it wasn't Mr. Johnson it'd have been Ms. Prime or—what's that friend of Skillet's name? Paper Don. Never been able to stand him. Could've been me. Nobody's too young to be out there howling down the modern world. The modern world is insane."

"But you keep watch for him."

"Folks know if something's wrong."

"Then the world makes sense," Dennis countered.

"Tell you this about Ophelia and Regina," said Lisa, tapping the side of her nose. "When Gina hit seventeen, side by side they were about the most beautiful pair. Almost pass for sisters. Acted it, too."

"Where'd they live?"

"White trash neighborhood down the block and around the corner from us. After the boom. We lived five miles east toward Clarksville Station. First she lived with me."

He remembered Skillet telling Regina about a scared white girl thinking to give her baby up one summer day.

"Couldn't have been easy."

Lisa mulled over all the things it could and should have been.

She caught Dennis' hesitation.

They returned to the living room. Lisa kept phone books and photo albums in a curio beside the sofa. The TV droned on. She pulled an old clothbound tome of a book out, the kind that attracts ghosts. She opened the book to a very specific page and handed it across to him.

"This is what she looked like."

A man and woman, posed to appear austere and unstoppable, in love and damn those who chose to oppose the kick they planted in the ass of society. Behind and around the man and woman: flowers, tall and full leafed. A botanical garden except everything seemed too well ordered. More likely someone's plant shop. Buds and blooms surrounded this slender white woman and this tall, serious-looking man.

They weren't smiling, both being old enough to know that the future might not leave much to smile about..

Ophelia was truly lovely. A lovely face. The impression might have owed something to the soft focus, air brushed quality of photos of the time. Ophelia had given her eyes to Regina (but every woman had her mother's eyes) and the same soft, dreamy patina of beauty hiding in the face.

The man looked like Dennis' grandfather, as every photo from this time looked like his grandfather. Brown, capable and tall, the kind of man who was only imposing when he needed to be, wearing his jaunty hat at an angle. Ophelia held hers in front of her pelvis. It always looked like Sunday in old pictures.

"She looks like an actress," he said. "She reminds me of," he prompted himself, digging at a face. Someone cool, but not Bacall. Someone winsome but not Garland. Sexy like only a woman in a black and white photo could be full of contrasts, textures and lighting.

"Wasn't she pretty?" Lisa asked.

Would he have desired her at that time if he'd been the one behind her, been some other black man who risked courting her? She did look like the kind of prize a black man, red man, brown man, even a white man would suffer the slings and arrows of outrageous fortune for. She was slightly taller than Regina. Looked like she might throw a punch if need be.

"That was in Ms. Hutchfield's flower shop. She was the only one this area had a decent camera; her and Charles, might as well say, had the first real photo studio in the whole state. You should've seen the line of black folks outside their place on Sundays."

"Poe and Hutchfield's?" he said, surprised. He'd seen the store downtown.

"That's hers."

"Who's Poe?"

"Dead a long time. She's got two more. The Hutchfield Triangle. Only one of the shops still sells flowers and takes pictures. Other two strictly develop."

He continued studying the picture, sneaking peeks at Regina's father from the peripheral: the Man Unspoken of; the Road Less Traveled; the Invisible Hand; the—what had Skillet said they called him?—Float. The tall mellow fellow. Finally he broke through this assemblage of thoughts. "He was a handsome man." That was safe. *He*, not "your brother". *A handsome man*, not "where is he?" Dennis glanced to see what kind of remembrance Lisa held behind her eyes.

Fond. After year after year in uncertainty, with the tinge of shame and blunt force of hatred, she remained his sister.

Through that tiny crack she allowed to pour as much as they needed of Grimm Nevills, the man whose photo existed only in her albums. About her brother it was said a forgiveness was extended which encompassed the length of God's true word and back. Didn't matter what he'd done. He was ego-less, motivated by love and curiosity. Black women silently offered to cheat on their men with him; white women risked glancing his way double. But did he know this? No. No, if Gloria said can you come by and check this piping for me, he'd frown and say didn't she want Skillet? No? OK. Maybe he'd show up. Most likely he wouldn't, seeing as Anna would try to grab him too. If not Anna, Maracell. If not Maracell those whores down by the creek when this town still had a serviceable creek. Grimm wasn't so innocent as to pretend obliviousness; it was more that he usually found something of more interest than sexing himself into oblivion. Ophelia and Grimm never told anybody how they met.

The family, meaning Grimm's, gradually adopted the consensus that the only way that white girl had got him was she followed his trail and went after him. Mama and Daddy died while Grimm went off to war (before he met Ophelia) but no one told him till he came home. It made sense at the time. They didn't want him getting shot worrying. Year after he came home is when he took up with the white girl, and since lynchings weren't from some ancient forgotten past, his sisters feared maybe he'd decided he didn't need to live much longer without parents. A black man might die one of two reasons: simply out of blackness or because he was black but had made love with a daughter of the wrong color. When folks are damned if they don't they usually go ahead and do. Grimm did.

And fell stupidly in love.

If the baby scared him away it'd be the only time duty of any type, to their knowledge, intimidated him.

If he left the earth because of the second reason black men die then it was the first his sisters had known him to abandon the strength of family for the danger of running alone.

If he didn't leave, if the suitcase and few missing clothes meant something else, if his not leaving a note was sign that something was wrong, if he was dead...well, no need to tell the boy this, but if he was dead, he was dead.

"We've had people trying to find him for years. Not anymore. Far as we're concerned he never left."

"I understand," Dennis said.

"I do wish Mama and Daddy were still with us."

"...no other way..."

"He's coming back," said Dennis.

"No other way. No other—" Johnson's voice, though strong, carried a tremulous note.

"No other way you gonna see God," the voice implored. Jesus Johnson came closer, mingling into the small talk Lisa kept up while she wondered what was wrong.

His voice, which continued even closer, mounted her porch steps, respectfully softened to a murmur, and quieted to nothing. He rang her doorbell.

Lisa answered. He looked through her. Both his hands were clasped as though he held a trembling butterfly. He didn't have his stick. Without a word Lisa brought him inside.

"Mr. Johnson?"

"They been in my house," he whispered, cracking with the effort of trying to remember the right way to cry.

She sat him down.

"Girl, you got some goodness cookin' up in here," he congratulated absently. It smelled so good it'd created a memory in him, leading to her house after seeing his side door ajar—the wood of the frame slightly cracked and jutting like bone—sent him on this moment of wandering. The gray sky, the quiet neighborhood, a silent wilderness. Lifeless except for the escaping scents surrounding Lisa Nevills' home. "I need Skillet to fix my door," he said. He noticed Dennis. "No other way," he said.

"No other way," Dennis returned.

"Mr. Johnson, you didn't see anybody?"

Jesus Johnson shook his head.

"Ain't heard your dog barking." With a full head of steam Johnson's dog could be heard for blocks around.

"Dead."

"I'll call the police," Lisa said.

"I need Mr. Dumas to fix my door. That's all, please." His expression was exactly that of a painful shard of bone jutting into the open air, a quick, precise breakage.

"Which house is it?" Dennis already had his cell phone out, heading for the door, sprinting for the address Lisa gave him, calling the police, declining to call Regina, afraid of having to step around a big dead dog but damned if he'd let a pitiable old man feel life was nothing but caprice and abandon. He circled the house, surveying for neighbors. It was a cloudy, gloomy day, and if Johnson's neighbors weren't indoors watching *Life's Work* they were asleep or well away from any windows. No witnesses.

The dispatch operator advised against entering the house. Having no weapon but himself, he would have to do. He entered.

Whoever had done this left behind a dead dog. Probably poisoned.

With malice aforethought.

They knew the home and occupant's schedule.

With plans to prey.

Therefore whomever had done this was certainly not inside.

Therefore whomever had done this suspected, as the world always will, that weird old men are consummate hoarders of valuables.

"No other way!"

"Confess yourself to Heaven." Dennis muttered this order to the house's unseen new presence as he climbed a short track of stairs to the kitchen: straight ahead the kitchen, to the right the dark basement. Given any chance that there was someone hiding down there best to leave that one avenue open.

He remembered the stout walking stick dropped by the elder beneath the bones of the door. Before crossing two steps into the kitchen he doubled back to retrieve it. He heard the first distant siren, probably not even for this home but still, he heard the first distant siren as his hand firmly gripped the stick.

The siren screamed its insistent, governing-body rational thought in quiet counterpoint to the god-like mix of adrenalin and blood heating the outer layers of Dennis' skin: "When we arrive you truly don't want to be in the house."

He backed out of the yard, past the modest fence that encompassed the entire home, eight poles with metal stretched between them, no barbs, he'd even painted the fence. Powder blue. The color of God's floating beards.

Those beards were dark now, heavy with contemplation overhead, turning this fence, this house, into a forlorn history.

Johnson's dog had died not too far from its doghouse. Dennis studied her house. The same powder blue. Her master had leftover paint.

Who would be so stupid as to kill a dog when it could've died loudly on the front lawn?

Or better, who had cased this neighborhood sufficiently to know the who, how, when and why of robbing Jesus Johnson's house with impunity?

"Mother*fuck*!" Dennis snarled, so suddenly angry that before he knew it he spun like a discuss thrower, snatched up a rock and let it fly…straight through one of Jesus Johnson's upper windows. The glass, struck on one of its tender spots, paused just a second before loudly and decisively shattering.

"Damn." *Now* curtains were being moved slightly aside, as though a single breeze filtered through the interiors of these suddenly vigilant homes.

Dennis called Lisa, and then sat on the curb to wait for the police to arrive.

While one of the officers was double checking to make sure he had correctly assumed the position, the other, a stoic woman who actually made the clunky police trousers look good, pushed the redial on his phone and began speaking with Lisa, who hurriedly put Jesus Johnson on the phone. When the officer hung up and actually said, "Your story checks out," Dennis realized that there was indeed order to the universe.

The other officer, who didn't make her pants look good, apologized, told him to relax, and even rubbed the imprint of the fence on his palms for a second.

"Window wasn't broke," Jesus Johnson said after he and Lisa arrived. He stared Dennis' way reprovingly before sizing up the two black women with guns and uniforms. Capable, he decided. Capable. Someone into whose hands he might crawl without shame. "No other way," he stammered, crying now at the wholly different shame of these two extra witnesses to not his but the Lord's shame.

"We'll go in first before we bring you inside," the first officer said, checking Johnson's ID card Lisa had handed over.

"No other way..." he mumbled.

"I've been here fifteen minutes. There's nobody in there," said Dennis.

The second officer smiled his way and unclipped her flashlight. "Stay away from rocks," she said.

Later, while Regina soaped the back of his neck and asked, "So what'd they take?" he sighed and nudged off the hot water tap with his toe.

"Nothing but assumptions. Killed his dog because they thought it protected something." He sighed again. "We left Skillet with him." Without warning he slapped his palm against the water. "Motherfuck!"

"You're cleaning this water off the floor."

He sighed again.

"I brought him home for dinner," Lisa told her sister Marion over the phone. Marion's husband was in the background asking about his inflatable doughnut. "Not one word the whole time he ate."

"You wouldn't want to talk either."

"At least he ate. Dennis didn't say anything either."

"They've got to be men."

"That's a shame."

"Dennis said he planned on finding out who did it."

"What does he do?"

"Don't know," Lisa said, then added quickly to cut her sister off, "Ain't worrying about it. Gina's got enough sense not to give us reason to stomp her."

Marion clucked her teeth. "Pitiful neighborhood watch. Half can't see, half can't hear."

"I asked the police why we can't see more patrols through here. This is, what, the eighth robbery since—"

"Ophelia died."

"Yep. About the beginning of the year. Obviously word's out this area's quick, easy pickings."

"Ain't like there's a scarcity of suspects," Marion remarked. "Seems like everyday somebody's taking the time to walk about."

"Two new drug houses on Lemay. Side by side."

"Lord."

"Whites this time. Ain't seen that much trash in one place since the Klan." Both women burst into raucous laughter recalling how lunatic Lisa, under a full moon, had been to spike a Klan's midnight celebration with enough diuretic to give everybody the runs a good two days.

"Don't come through town messing with a former pharmacist's daughter."

"Hee hee."

"Yes, ma'am."

"Anyway..."

The dog, Maya, had been buried. Jesus Johnson was adamant about that. Dennis saw to the labor before the old man picked up the shovel himself. An investigation interested Johnson about as much as finding gold two inches below Maya's grave. No fat bottomed police officer or her partner would tell him otherwise. Absolutely not.

"Well, who called the police?" fat bottom demanded.

"I told you I did," Dennis said, which earned him a warning glance from nice bottom.

"Did they handcuff you, baby?" Regina asked with a playful pout, straddling him in bed with firm hold of his wrists, feeling him lengthen despite his pretense of humoring her. She bent to him, dangling her nipples at his neckbone. "My sweet," she whispered warmly beside his ear, "stoic," and a kiss on the upper curve of that ear, "husband."

Suddenly time stopped. Suddenly there was so little left, so little of anything. Perfect stasis. He'd never understood stasis before. Suddenly all of life *shlooped* into the densest point of clarity and focus he would ever know. Not even when he died sixty-two years later held by the adult stepson from his second wife would the fine prick of God trying to get his attention resonate so deeply. Suddenly this sweet woman atop him was the most important thing there ever would be and he was charged with her protection to the exclusion of all else, but damn it, charged without his consent!

Which, if nothing else, was the nature of stoicism.

Husband.

It was his moment of realization when he *knew* that it was his duty to feel he must change the world for her.

He breathed deeply, relaxing through a mouth gone slack, lips slightly agape to feel the pleasant rush of confusion in wisdom. His breath rustled the ends of her hair. If he opened his eyes now he'd probably see a halo behind her so he kept his eyes closed. His wife's name was Regina, and she was no angel. A woman didn't need to be an angel to be perfect. Ygrane was no angel. Cleopatra was no angel. Nefertiti was no angel.

Regina nibbled the borderline where his skull met his neck, causing his body to involuntarily shudder and penis to spasm. Then it was quickly inside her.

Regina was no angel.

"Who told you to kill a dog? Fucking beautiful German Shepherd. Shit, boy, you don't just go around killing somebody's dog. You don't think somebody woulda bought that dog? You didn't get nothin' from that house you couldn'ta got from anywhere else that didn't have a dog. Ya little fourteen-year-old ass." Pendle took a moment to consider smacking Norton for effect. "And using anti-freeze."

Wasn't anybody going to consider the boy's patience in feeding the dog anti-freeze several days ago? The boy mumbled, "Made it sick enough to leave me alone."

"Be leavin' a lotta folks alone. Now nab'll be all over them old folks a good week. Shit, boy, don't you know we got elections comin' up? Take ya ass on to school, fool, learn something."

Norton stood from the rickety card table. "Just like that? I'm out?"

"This look like the Mafia to you? You wasn't never *in!*"

Norton's mother, broken by her son's destructive ignorance, had put him out four months ago. He hesitated, hoping Penny's ire was for show only.

Rial Pendle—Penny—glanced up from his bowl of cereal, brows arched as though wondering why in hell this little boy was still there. The boy hesitated longer, waiting for Penny to say something. All Penny did was look at him, a crocodile's flat stare of curious disinterest.

Norton dug in his pockets for the crumpled bags of drugs he'd bought with Jesus Johnson's two watches and extra bass portable stereo. Penny was eating from the box of Sweetnut Flakes Norton swiped as an afterthought from the top of the old man's refrigerator. Norton loved that cereal.

Damn.

The scraggly boy desultorily placed all three bags on the table, deliberately out of Penny's reach. Just because of a dog he was cut out of his piece when Penny turned around and sold these drugs four times their price to some dumb ass out in the suburbs.

Penny, though, was thinking that he was either going to have to stay low for a week or both sell and steal in the burbs, but only a fool stole out in boonie land on a regular basis.

"This is why I can't stand a greedy motherfucker," he said coldly.

"Man, all I got was three bags!" Norton said, misunderstanding. This was Penny telling him he was straight up boonie-baby stupid with his mama's tittie milk still on his lips. If not for the fact that he'd loaned some of his bullets to a friend, with only two in the chamber to last till next week, Norton would have popped it out for this scrawny fuck to define for him the mettle of man.

Penny shouted the boy's pride down. "I'm talking about the dog! Don't tell nobody about the dog!"

Norton looked away angrily. "Man, why you keep fuckin' with me?" he said softly.

"School yourself, boy." Penny glanced into his bowl to see where to shovel his spoon next. They never put enough nuts in Sweetnut Flakes. Crunching his clusters, he asked Norton, "Who's gonna have your babies if you ain't got sense enough to know when to leave shit alone?"

Norton left, thinking of kicking at the scroungy dog that hung outside Penny's squat, considering calling his mother up just to make her dread that she might be forced to take him back, but neither option offered substantial relief. He paused on the sidewalk. Still early morning. Kids carried backpacks. Little kids. Third through fifth grades.

Fuck Moms and her backpack waiting at home for him. "Mamas is the most stupid things in the *entire* world," his friend Ralph had told him sliding the four bullets into their holes. Ralph lived at home. "These cheap ass guns from Penny Ante ain't shit."

"Like a rotary phone," Norton laughed.

"What?"

"Phones with the holes in 'em, man."

"Grandmother. They be havin' us and don't know what the fuck to do."

"You got that one girl pregnant," Norton felt to remind him.

"You said no to pussy?"

"Not recently."

"Oh, young man."

Norton pursed his lips. "You a year older than me."

Norton wandered opposite the stream of backpacked kids. Which of the network of squats should he go to next? It was too cold to wonder for too long. Matter of fact, the first few flakes of a peculiar season decided right then to descend, spiraling like paratroopers, entering this gray morning to the delight of the school kids. One small boy remained in place, gauging the bare November wind, patiently waiting for a flake he'd observed to trajectory to the landing pad of his small outstretched hand. There was a gap between the children ahead and the children behind him; the boy, tiny in his mother-wrapped bundle, was alone. "Kids get happy at nothing," Norton pronounced to himself, noticing the way the chill wind coiled his own breath outward in dragon spirals. He made an *O* of his lips and blew a stable stream, imagining the sound effects of a giant radioactive dinosaur and the city toppling under its clawed flat feet.

"What if God is a woman, Ralph?"

"God ain't no woman."

"You really believe in God?" asked Norton.

"Yeah."

Norton hoped Ralph was around, but Ralph's dumb butt was always out for revenge that for some reason never materialized. It was like people knew he was coming and they either took off to ignore him or had somebody else beat him up en route to give him more pertinent concerns.

"You believe in God?" Ralph asked in turn.

Norton responded with a shrug.

Ralph tucked the small gun that had no workable safety into the waist of his underpants and covered it over with his shirttail. "Who else you think be laughin' at us all the time?" he said.

"I don't get laughed at," said Norton.

"You got a complex. Meet me 'round Sweetheart's Friday."

"When?"

"I'ma try to get there before dark."

"When?" Norton pressed, not planning to spend all week waiting to waste Friday for Ralph not to show up.

"Six, fool." He shrugged into his jacket and zipped up. Carrying his bike to the door he called over his shoulder, "Peace, fool."

"Peace."

Snow now swirled around Norton's head and he blew it away in puffs. *Penny ain't have to keep my cereal.*

I wonder what I look like sometimes, he thought.

Norton wandered from squat to squat, each time being turned away for waking folks up when someone bothered to answer that house's particular knock. Word traveled too fast. "Nothing for you today," came at him three different times. It seemed overnight he'd graduated from petty larceny to incompetent murder in the first; nickel and dime drug houses didn't have the *cajones* for that kind of grief, particularly when they were already on the police lists to be raided once every two months.

Today was Thursday. The money Penny'd given him for the theft itself would carry till Saturday, but that hardly meant the desire to spend it. Two bus rides later Norton knocked on Sweetheart's door. She never left before noon.

He disappointedly slurped down a bowl of cereal in her apartment: no oat and nut clusters, no almonds or mummified fruit bits, just flakes, pale yellow generic off the shelf already soggy shit, but he wasn't so unschooled as to voice or visibly complain. He ate his breakfast quietly while she fought several impulses to crawl back into bed. She gathered her pressing iron and holding spray.

"What you fixin' for dinner tonight?" he asked idly when she pulled a seat to the stove and proceeded to press her hair.

"Mama's thinkin' about Mexican. Toss off some tacos with that good gub'mint cheese!" She howled with laughter, burning herself. "Shit! Ow!"

He used to watch his mama do that, only with chemicals, not iron. Mama's friends sometimes came over and they'd all do the same thing, a bunch of loud black women treating their hair like each handful was a witch on a stake.

Hair parties. Sometimes her friends brought kids with them. Newborns, toddlers, four-year-olds running wild banging his toys against tables and floors till, glass-eyed, Norton had to walk out of the house and sit on the bottom step of the front porch, a twelve year old boy with too much on his mind.

"Wouldn't it be easier just to get wigs?" he said. Sweetheart ignored the crack. *Black women are crazy*, thought Norton.

White mothers, black mothers, single women, any woman thinking about having a kid and hair at the same time, all crazy. Ralph was right. Ralph was wise. Who else had everything figured out by fifteen? Penny was as clueless as they came. Sweetheart was good for snacks or a few minutes where nobody bothered you if you caught her in the right mood. The dealers he ran for, played lookout for, stole for, hadn't been able to tell him a thing about the world. Ralph, though, concisely summed everything Norton needed for placing blame.

Norton studied Sweetheart's slight body. She'd thrown a robe over her nightgown. She sat with her legs spread feet flat for stability while she held her elbows above her head. He imagined her pregnant as a test and instantly hated her.

Yep, that was it then. Mothers. Who in hell would *want* to have a kid? Hadn't been one yet in recorded history that had failed to grow up. They wouldn't stay babies. They'd grow up and be forever *looking* for something. He, himself, would never have a child.

He thought up a good one: Mothers ain't nothing but girls playing with baby dolls caught off guard.

He congratulated himself with another half bowl of cereal.

Sweetheart burned herself again. "It's too early to be doin' this!" she railed. The radio was giving its purchased news report. "Pop that CD in."

The tip of a torrent of love songs poured out.

"Don't you want me to do your hair?" she asked, dry cigarette bobbing in the crook of her mouth. "That bush baby 'fro ain't workin', son."

"My hair is cool. Ralph's supposed to be comin' round here tomorrow."

She shrugged. Didn't mean anything special far as she was concerned.

Norton waited till she left the room, then dug two dollars out his pocket and dropped them on the counter spot by the fridge as hospitality money. She returned dressed in a short black thing, straightened hair combed backward in an unruly mane. She offered her cheek to him; he kissed it, so used to the ritual that he was able to think about Penny while his lips touched her face.

For her strays the kiss was goodbye in case she never saw them again.

Bad news came that day to George Sumner. Dorsett and Callie, so concerned, hovered outside the open door of his greenhouse pacing the covered walkway that joined it to the house. George was far too old for carrying on. Last night they'd all received the news of his nurse's son's death, that woman who had become almost a second wife to him.

Callie broke the silent waves of dread Dorsett sent out each time Dorsett, with her failing eyes, peered through the heavy fronds of their father's jungle. She moved her younger sister aside with a tap on her arthritic shoulder and entered the jungle with the intent of seeing if he'd at least nibbled on the breakfast of fruits and cheese Dorsett set out earlier that morning.

She made sure to rustle enough leaves for composure. He always sat in the corner of the greenhouse which faced where the muse Thalia, nymph daughter of a hermit god, often appeared to quizzically regard this old man who found the time to sit in wait for her, who stared through the clear panes of his insect structure like a voyeur while she bathed her translucent feet in the pool of the gurgling rock fountain someone had cleverly designed to resemble a Grecian bath if

Grecian baths were naturally occurring. Sometimes instead of washing her feet she leaned back and watched the clouds float across what she refused to believe was not her father's sky. Her presence was not known to Callie or Dorsett.

To the old codger's credit he hadn't called out or summoned others to share this vision, and Thalia knew she was indeed a vision but where she came from visions were common; she couldn't fathom his continued fascination with her. Sometimes when she watched this old man, say ninety, white mottled forehead and thick wire glasses, gray hair combed to the back and wavy at the temples, she felt momentarily Elizabethan; he seemed to her full of dramas and authority.

Today he saw nothing, not because he wished to see nothing but because she wasn't there.

George hadn't touched the fruit. A piece of cheese appealed for mercy from the plate, its lower half truncated by one bite. The significance of food had been forgotten. George slumped over what he still called his writing desk even though his hands were past legibility. His face atop his hands, his eyes open, and the sun warmed him.

Callie smoothed what was left of his hair down, settling her weathered palm on the back of his head.

He knew his children's distinctive touches, and didn't stir. "Has Lois called?" he asked.

"No."

"Send her some food."

"You need to eat." She pushed the plate of fruits and cheese away. "Something hot."

"What time is it?" Somewhere in him he felt foolish talking to his daughter from the side of his face.

She told him.

"I've been in here since sunrise," he realized.

"We all grieve, Daddy." She smoothed the back of his head again. "George, you need to eat."

"When I'm hungry." His eyes traveled without concern over the russet stones of what he knew as the Muse's fountain. "Who's cooking?"

"Dorsett."

"Pancakes. My back hurts." He groaned upright and peered the great distance over his shoulder at his first child. She would be considered elderly herself but to him her round face glowed with youth. Though she was trying not to show it, that round face was tight with concern. He could only imagine how he looked: red sunken eyes, salt trail across the bridge of his thick nose. "I'd like some music," he said. "Some chanting. Through the entire house."

"When you come out for breakfast," Callie promised.

"I don't care who's chanting," he said, voice gaining. "Gregorian, Japanese traditional, Yoruba—no words, no people, pre-lingua…" A fresh glimpse of what might have happened to the boy struck him with vehemence. "I want this house to wail!"

Dorsett appeared beside Callie. She took the plate.

George looked at her. "I'm tired of thinking, dear. My assumptions are useless."

"Come have breakfast," Callie urged again, but he became agitated and shooed them out.

Dorsett sought the unthinking routine of the kitchen. Pancakes with warm cinnamon-apple compote would do well to draw him away from those plants.

Moments later haunting Scottish dirges bellowed through house and grounds, reaching George Sumner like a light scratch across the eye.

"Gods, girl, abet me, don't drown me."

He drew his recorder across the table. Lois wouldn't be pleased at pity.

The humidity and heat of the tropical garden soothed his joints. The commingled aromas of his plants distracted him from the omnipresent weaknesses of age. But his thoughts...

...the gods created no greater sufferance than the reception of bad news.

Lois was his transcriptionist as well as nurse. The following words, though, were not meant for her to hear. As he spoke, George didn't care one way or another if Thalia appeared outside among his hedges and manicured lawn. His view of the fountain and water were undisturbed. For now, the rock and the water were perfect reasons to stare into space.

The dirge swelled abruptly and at that moment he loved the devotion of both his daughters so immensely that his throat caught. He paused, searched for tissues, found none since he'd forgotten them. He wiped his nose on his sleeve.

Whenever he became truly angry his mind turned inward to address the memory of his ex-wife Andrea: *I care too much, do I?*

"I think about violence," the old man told the recorder, its digital memory soaking the words up.

"The sickening, hateful stupidity of it. Mindless violence. God's in its heaven, Andrea, while we all die. It becomes so very, very hard to give a shit." Lois frowned on cursing but he'd heard her use a few choice words of her own. Life was not nice anymore.

It had likely never been.

"Lois' youngest son was murdered. The body was found only yesterday. A shot to the head. He was twenty-eight. I don't know when Lois will return to herself. Damnation's bloodied edge! I didn't know the young man, don't know what he might have run across outside the fact that he'd suddenly decided to quit teaching. Lois asked me about that. I'm not choked like I am, sad and dark like I am, angry, so damn very ugly angry as I am out of forced grief for the loss of the child. I feel because Lois must be consumed in fires. Angry because she is my friend and she is in pain. Because some asshole killed Lois Wayne's son."

He drew a breath.

He'd written in *Sumner's Guide to Primates* the inescapable conclusion that it was due time the world ended.

"I knew I was right."

That woman, who harmed no one, now had to sleep with the word *murder* every night the rest of her life.

"An idiot, primitive, misbegotten shit might kill me or one of mine," he nearly whispered in case Andrea's God was listening for ideas. "An idiot with a gun. Or a knife. Or a bat. Or heavy boots. But probably a gun, because the minds that love and need pain don't think. If no thought, no conscience. No care. People kill people, guns don't. Wasn't that the slogan? We are reduced…" He was about to sigh but stifled it.

What use is sighing when you'd rather growl and scream?

I have felt the narrowing of the eyes and the low growl of a thing unnamed.

Carefully and very deliberately he placed the recorder directly in his line of sight atop the polished desk. An impulse to smash it against his reflection had taken him too suddenly.

"You see, Andrea, I'm responsible. Why aren't you? Each damnation we suffer, *I* suffer. Inside where it has no voice but, gods, does it make its presence known." Now he sighed. Lois wouldn't be pleased with him at all. Ire had no place in honoring the dead.

Instead, he decided to build a children's park somewhere in the world with his name on it and hire policemen with *big* guns to stand at each corner of its gates. Let the primitives pout and call him a spiteful old bastard, even a rich prick. Let them cry for that piece of joy.

Do you know what I'll say?
The killer in me is the killer in you.

By the next Spring Norton never saw Ralph again but he did, for right now, get to meet—following Sweetheart to the hardware barn for traps which hid the traps under a plastic casing so the mouse's snapped body wasn't seen—this spaz who pointed him in the direction of a hot dog man who gave him a free dog, weird-necked white guy who didn't look friendly at all.

Norton thought the man would say something along the lines of: "How in sweet fuck does that affect you and me?" but then, the way Sweetheart was talking to Shaffer made it seem like the spaz was all right enough, and if he was then a free dog from this old hump working a teenager's job didn't seem too much to ask.

"You seventeen yet?" the hot dog man asked.

Sweetheart hadn't gone grocery shopping. Norton hungrily bit into the bread and ersatz meat. "I'm seventeen."

Robert Michilane appraised this young man, laughing inwardly.

"College bound?"

"Air Force."

"They'll cut your hair." He tossed Norton a bag of chips. "Mother must be proud."

To him Sweetheart probably looked like every black kid's ma; Norton, though, simply kept chewing.

"Stand here to the side."

A thin, rakish carpenter came up and bought three dogs.

"They teach you about war in the Air Force."

"I plan to fly." Norton finished the dog and tore open the chips. He looked about for Sweetheart and Sanchez or Pancho Villa or whatever his name was.

"You haven't told me your name," Robert said.

"My bad. Kenny," he said with a nod.

Robert returned the nod. "Mickey," he said. "That's M-I-C-K-E-Y. I've noted," he went on, "as for defeat, you defeat anybody, people been defeated? People defeated are always given the means to keep destroying themselves. You smoke?"

"Naw."

"Good for you. Let old people be self-destructive."

Norton smiled broadly.

Robert cocked a quizzical brow at him.

"You sound like a Nation of Islam brother talkin' down the forty ounce nation," Norton said out the side of his smirk.

"You drink? Nobody cares about the city. Islam brothers know all about war. When's the last time you saw a billboard for hard liquor in the burbs?"

"Don't get to the burbs too often, man."

"You fish?"

"Naw."

"We'll go fishin' next summer."

"Right."

"Here comes your ma."

Thalia, the beatific Muse of Comedy and Idyllic Poetry, was also known in some cultures as *the Liar*.

She credited among her achievements inspiring Paul McCartney and John Lennon to write *Rocky Raccoon*.

"No one is saved," she whispered, letting the cosmic winds sweep the words around the entire globe. The angel observing her ignored this inspiration, just as she ignored the angel. The only thing with time more ephemeral than an angel's was a gnat lost in a bat cave. Moreover, angels even resembled clouds of gnats; over time, Thalia and her eight sister muses had grown accustomed to completely negating these clouds from their notice, the better to inspire people in true muse fashion: like a handkerchief disingenuously dropped from the hands of a southern belle.

8

Nothing Ends, Ophelia

This time the news said an abortion clinic was bombed. Two people dead: the receptionist and a woman arriving early for her morning counsel. One person seriously injured: a man who'd been in such a rush he hadn't even noticed he'd parked in front of a *Women's Health* clinic, hurrying to his car before the meter expired. Two shards of brick lodged squarely in the side of his neck where his scarf had slid down.

In the parking lot behind the building one lucky woman, saved by hesitance, trembled uncontrollably, hand glued to the stick shift, body frozen in the midst of the bomb's decision to have her child, a child she would now raise but in deliberate miserable fashion. Her sister beside her found God.

"The blast was directed toward the street!" an angry fire fighter observed later in disgust, turning momentarily away from the reporter's simplistic inquiries. He was soot covered and sick of reporters. He pointed out the scene, accusing the viewing public. "Only grace is whoever did this set it to blow early morning. Je-sus!"

"He screams out Jesus on the national news, I mumble one expletive—what'd I say?" Ron Chiamp, host of *Life's Work*, asked his wife.

"You said goddamn."

"Oh."

"This country is about to rip in half," Regina said, tightening tiny screws in Dennis' beat up glasses.

Dennis remained uncommunicative since Jesus Johnson's robbery last week. His wife had yet to hear a single utterance of value from him, nothing to indicate he was more to her than just the function of heart and bones. What she couldn't know—and he had no intention of telling—was he was gathering his strength, appealing to everything the world didn't as yet know to step forward and make itself known. Quickly. One everything at a time would do, and perhaps if he thought enough, one would. One in particular. Someone irrefutable.

Jesus was on Mars making it hospitable to human life.

Dennis James rubbed at his eyes as though they were tired or wrong, but there was no sense in praying to be wrong anymore against the advances of modern news. The routine Regina implemented of turning on the TV after dinner quietly bled him. For four days he hadn't said anything against it, preferring the solitude of sitting mutely beside his wife. Pathos was not unheard of in the gathering of strength.

Besides, if he thought about her long enough, about *her*, if he nagged at the recollection till she frowned somewhere on earth and looked over her shoulder, if he nagged and nagged until she bolted upright and shouted, "All right!" and revealed herself to everyone as a true mystery, then the news could be beaten. The woman who lived in three bodies.

Why didn't I ask your name?

"Please turn it off," he said numbly.

She did.

"Catalogs of reasons we shouldn't exist," he said.

Wait.

"There is nothing so important TV can't minimize it."

Wait.

She gave him his glasses.

"We should move, Gina."

He sighed deeply.

"There's nowhere to go," she gently helped him realize.

"Where does your friend go?"

"My friend?"

"The artist."

She smiled and proceeded to massage his bunched muscles. A forest. A clearing in which to rest. A place where the grass didn't bite. She kissed the nape of Dennis' neck. "You want him to draw you?"

"Yeah."

The smell and texture of his crinkly hair drew her lids closed. She batted troubling thoughts away from his head. "We should get a new frame for my portrait," she suggested.

They did a day later. Dennis bought it: a sheet of glass with four tiny brackets holding the charcoal sketch in place against a wood backing. It hung in their bedroom like this:

———————————————

———————————————

Which is to say it was a mirror, stared at in a penetrating way that made Dennis wonder why he was staring. It hung on the wall opposite a brand new bed.

Nights when he turned out the lights he had the habit of studying the sketch's detailed simplicity. Every night its image superimposed itself over darkness. The realism on his wife's forest face left him with the impression of illicitly sleeping with two women. In dreams, he was never quite sure which he preferred.

Thanksgiving passed by, thankless. He dreamed a lot.

December rounded and the predictions of weatherman William Pounast marched through, late (and forgotten) but practically accurate. Inches of wet, heavy snow rose, froze, melted, rose, froze, melted over a week long cycle ending on a Monday with the cycle at froze. The wind snapped like a towel.

Roads visibly giggled at cars trying to maintain a sense of dignity while skidding.

And a somewhat moot winter ice advisory was issued.

"Are we the only ones who made it?" Harper asked. Angela Carmen and Regina stood behind twin clouds of chocolate steam. He pointed out Angela's hips. "How many layers you wearin'? Looks like you put on ten pounds."

"Why aren't you at home with your daughter?" asked Regina.

"Why aren't you at home with your husband? Thanks," to Angela handing him a steaming cup. He glanced over the surface of the doughnut table, naked and shivering without the weight of lopsided desserts.

"Least I finally got more ass than you," said Angela.

"Simply because I'm beautiful." His fingers praised the warmth of the filled cup. "Since we're the only ones, I say we don't do jack till somebody else shows up."

"Plus take long breaks," Regina pointed out.

"I think I got frostbite opening this place up," Angela said.

"You wanna warm 'em top or bottom?" Harper asked.

"I knew there was a reason I slid to work," said Regina. "Harper, you didn't drop your daughter off at work, did you?" She suspected he had but wanted to hear it for herself.

His delighted grin answered.

"I'm glad I don't have you for a father."

"Folks might raise eyebrows."

She shrugged behind her steam. "Not everybody has a father." Blowing into her cup sent up a welcome rush of chocolate.

"That bombing, the man who got killed, he had four kids. My sister knew him," Angela said, then cast her eyes down as though she'd spoken ill of the dead. She looked at them both to be sure they realized this was not meant for retelling.

"She went to college with him. He was a lawyer last time they talked. Four girls."

Harper apologetically admitted he didn't know the man had died.

"We shouldn't have come in to work," Angela said. She wanted to get her coat and go home.

"We're here," said Harper. "Where'd you leave off Friday?"

"That in there."

"I'll do this in here. You got those over there, Regina?"

"I got those over there."

"This might be the only productive day of work this company ever sees," Harper remarked.

On Friday the bombers delivered informational packets to the impatient receptionists of each of the thirty-six major television networks. They contained blast pictures, including one with the fireman who'd been interviewed at the scene. No one put two and two together that the bomber could have been a member of the press. Accompanying the pictures was a two paragraph mission statement full of uptight verbiage and a surprising self-acknowledgment of moral posturing: Yes, they claimed to love and want to protect life itself, but please let's be realistic: the love of a good steak and fries had to include its opposite, the death of some meat and a few potatoes.

The local news buffoons and the national news shills, every affiliated station of the thirty-six major networks as a matter of course displayed truncated bits of the envelopes' contents as repeatedly as appeared responsible, so much so that the fireman began to feel like a pre-martyred hero living on borrowed time. Even though his face wasn't visible in the picture the entire country knew it was him. He quickly became the heroic symbol of life, i.e., dutiful yet angry.

Ron Chiamp, while the news was on, sat across from his wife and faced the screen without really seeing it, fantasizing about being sucked off by his co-host, Charlene Roget.

His co-host, Charlene Roget, completed the synchronicity of the moment by fantasizing about making it with a woman. Any woman. Lesbianism had been in vogue pretty continuously. Directors loved vogue. She might do either one intense nude scene or a bunch of small non-titillating nude scenes in order to break away from the silly vacuity of gameshow celebrity. A lesbian scene automatically assured her of breakout status. The news was on in her house too but since she was already fully abreast of what was going on— since she personally knew who was behind the bombings— (even last year's theater parking lot bombing; same group but different objective) and agreed with them whole-heartedly, she ignored everything.

How would it feel, she wondered instead, to plant one on some woman's soft lips and finally get the hell away from Ron Chiamp?

Regina Nevills argued with Dennis James (granted he was as progressive as the next male but, unadmittedly, it rasped a bit she hadn't taken his name); not quite argued but adamantly fussed about the way he left her basement in disarray. He'd gone and stacked each book that belonged to a library—and to him more than one was shameful—on the floor next to the bookcase.

So she fussed that he had no clue what she was trying to do. The specific books she pilfered transcended ownership. They were vital to her well-being.

"Oh, please."

"Yours if you don't get them back."

"There's a sacred trust between library and user," he said, putting the books back. "Like this one here, the monkey book."

Before he could say anything else she asked him if he thought they had married too quickly.

"Yeah."

Then should we change it?

"No," he said, feeling again that unbidden magnificent blooming within which told him that she, of all women, was truly amazing.

"Me neither." She was thinking of old age. The end of things. Ask not who it tolls for, it tolls for thee.

The doorbell rang.

Dennis remained in the basement looking around at nothing in particular.

He remembered a movie he'd seen ages ago about a quartet of trolls. They'd spent a good part of the movie watching the heroine bathe. She often, and unknowingly, thwarted them by flicking on lights at the right moments.

The scary thing was that they didn't want to kill her. Their claws and unsettling appearances: shock value. What was truly unsettling was that they *wanted* her, maniacally, because she was other and they could not abide that. She had to become like them. Four trolls were hell bent on homogeneity. Trolls always lived in basements like this which women tried to make over as living spaces.

He didn't hear any talking upstairs but felt wind, cold and annoying, curlicue about his ankles. It was way past season for standing in the doorway chatting. There wasn't a salesman alive who'd risk a winter pitch, even this state's mild winters. Even religious nuts tended to forget God's graces during the months when sunlight served only to point out how cold the white bright snow would forever be.

He glanced at the bookshelf.

Somebody tipped off the police about her.

One of the reasons I love you, he recalled somewhat inaccurately, *is you steal library books.*

Besides which, she was just going to pick up fussing where she left off.

A full two minutes passed. He avoided thinking he'd better check on her, because people in movies who thought like that tended to meet up with axes, knives, or teeth.

The nearer the front door, the colder the house. Strong gusts of winter kept the storm door from shutting and sent rushes of dying snowflakes into the carpeting. Past the wide-open door *Outside* crammed its weight against the frame, weight of blue sky, weight of warmed houses, the mass of brightness, the invisible gravity of the wind inhaling Dennis' clouds of breath.

Pride kept him from calling for her. He leaned his head out and searched the length of the block.

Even as he started through the house for sign of her something about the ordinary nagged at him to return to the door.

For some reason there was an excess of weight to that bright wintry vista.

It wasn't that large a house for a disappearance.

It took only moments to rush scattershot through the house before the weight clicked and drew him back to the open door.

A swath of snow was neatly mown by the outward arch of the storm door through the drifts, but there were no tracks in the snow on the actual steps. Not even on the walkway. (It had made no sense to Dennis to shovel while snow plodded steadily.)

Snow that continued its mechanical falling, mute, indifferent and howlingly existential.

"Regina!"

He locked the door. She wasn't in the living room. "Who rang the doorbell?" he interrogated the passing empty rooms as though they withheld information. "Where's Regina?" he asked the complicit small eyes in the bedroom sketch.

She believed we'd all seen at least one thing we weren't supposed to see.

Sheer stupidity to think his idle thoughts of trolls had conjured up some kind of irony.

Hell, he knew precisely how his DVR and microwave worked.

She was in the house.

But someone had rung the bell.

The lights were on. The clocks were functioning. Four minutes had passed since her mounting the basement steps to him stopping himself from reaching for the phone.

"She's in this house. Regina!" Closets, bathroom, kitchen, attic, hallway, sunroom, beneath the bed...basement.

She couldn't have gotten past him into the basement without his having seen her.

But he'd been through the whole house—including peering at the undisturbed snow of the backyard—except the basement, which he couldn't go back into now. As he'd done with the doorway, he leaned his head turtle-like into the arch of the basement landing. He called loudly for her, with just the hint of if you're down there how'd you get there?

No answer. He turned quickly and bumped into her.

"Where the hell were you?" He held her by her upper arms, his heart racing. "Gina?" She trembled; he felt it in his palms without seeing it in her eyes or body. The barest shared oscillation traveled the length between them. He shook his head; for a blink he thought he'd seen himself moving through the kitchen for the front door. Shaking his head dispelled the vision but not the tenuous physical impression that he was still heading for that door.

Gina was here, held by him.

"Gina, where were you?"

Her mother was at the door.

"What the fuck!" He jumped back, releasing her, shivering free of the oscillations and the ghost images his wife fed him.

"Mama," she whispered, looking at the floor, "locked herself out of the house when I was fifteen." She stared into him as though he was supposed to understand something more about these words. "I think about her all the time."

No reason to wait for him to speak. He hadn't been there, not then and not now. "Mama locked herself out of this house. She got pissed because I was on the phone and didn't realize till she'd rung the bell three times that she was the one ringing it. She was *freezing* when I let her back in. I remember."

All he could think to do was look at her and hope that she saw the same kitchen he did, the one they stood in, but her thoughts were furrowed off to one side; she chewed her lip in deep remembrance of something that happened only moments ago.

"I looked, Gina."

"I'm cold."

"I'm cold," she repeated. "She got cold and mad and told me to open the damn door, only time she cussed at me. She went to get the mail, no coat, just slippers." Regina snorted a mad laugh, eyes slipping away again. "I'm cold!"

"Come here," he said. He rubbed her shoulders, leading her away from the basement, quickly through the living room, ignoring the house's questions about its matron and straight to the bedroom. He pulled the powder blue comforter from the bed and wrapped her inside it, sitting her on the bed and himself beside her. He rubbed her through the cocoon. The oscillations were tenuous; even leading to the bedroom it wasn't difficult convincing himself that the feelings and snatches of imagery were of his own making, no different than the way the house had seemed about to swallow him one night last summer.

Best not to think on that.

Instead he rubbed her and whispered her name. Her breathing had quickened. The phone. If she was going into shock…

God, why can't they just hear me, he thought, praying his thoughts into someone's head, an aunt who should have felt the panic of blood under her niece's skin.

He told her he was calling Lisa.

"No." Her eyes were slowly returning. "I need a bath. Turn on all the lights." She curled away from him and lay atop the bed.

She couldn't stretch out in the tub, not until after she'd hugged her knees a few minutes. The water steamed. For a moment the wavering air made her wonder if her mother was present. Regina was afraid and contrite at the desire to slide her bottom forward and sink her stomach, breasts, and neck so deeply under unscented waters she'd never be seen again.

Through the splash of the hot water tap she kept hearing Dennis asking *Where were you*, irritatingly as though he couldn't see her standing right in front of him, *Where were you* as though she had no right to be other than seen by him, *Where were you* louder and louder until it eclipsed the doorbell and became the threatening banging of fists and she told Jonathan to wait.

Ophelia stormed in like the embodiment of winter sickness, too enraged to say anything to her daughter who'd been on the phone with that *boy* for too damn long.

"Ma, Jonathan Hammer died five years after you got locked out. It's not right to speak ill of the dead."

"I *am* dead, girl!"

"Ma?" Regina wanted to be patient. "Don't you remember he was my best friend?"

"I remember everything!" Ophelia shrieked. Dead, she suddenly remembered everything. Glaringly. Dark skinned Jonathan Hammer. Grown up from the quietly mischievous boy her daughter played with to the slouchily handsome teenager who certainly had learned the ways to make a daughter pregnant or fall in love with him, losing all sight of a mother's plans, effectively creating a hole in a daughter's life.

Girls had terrible trouble with holes. Reverend Daville wouldn't tell Ophelia that that was God's true curse.

Regina relinquished herself to the water. The tub lapped at her chin. She breathed the steam, eyes closed to leave her body open to the sensation of a bath drawn for the sake of water. She tried to clear her mind of thoughts and scenarios but Ophelia wouldn't let her be.

"I have his scarf, Mama!"

Silence. The water lapped, creating a shore out of her body in the malleable darkness behind her closed lids.

It wasn't Jonathan's fault that Ma got locked out of the house.

Leave the dead to rest.

"I'm catching pneumonia because you're on the phone? I think not. Tell that boy—" part of Regina cringed whenever Mama used that word—"that you have to go."

Regina remained holding the front door.

"Damn it, girl, lock that door!" Ophelia stalked off, heading straight for the bathroom to splash her face with warm water; while in there, deciding to draw a bath and forget about making dinner for a while. To forget that Skillet had earlier overheard her agreeing with somebody over the phone that the black neighborhoods were in dire need of the civilizing influence of white folk. To forget that brief look he gave her as though she and nothing else had become the most disappointing thing on earth.

She couldn't forget.

Even the water streaming into Ophelia's tub was courtesy of Skillet. A repaired hot water tank.

Ophelia died under a square of sunlight, now even knew who killed her, knew his family, his history, his future. She knew there were many of her still wandering lost, but every spirit, out of all the ghostly shades of oneness, possesses that *one* which knows its moment.

She remembered. She remembered trapping her daughter inside remembrance, engulfing her in the slowed down dimension the forgetful dead disappear into, that fraction of a second which placed them just a little behind the common universe's heartbeat.

Oh, God, I had no idea what life is, fretted Ophelia Nevills independent of memory, unchained from repetition, autonomous enough now to observe her daughter, a grown woman, older than this frozen Ophelia sublimely ashamed of every decision of her life, the one with death forced on her by herself decades in the future who hadn't the inclination to eat and exercise properly to prevent her life ending the first time her heart demanded something of her. To Ophelia at thirty-two, Regina—an image seen through two layers of water, one the actual water her daughter soaked in, the other of death itself—had grown to look so much more like some other person, some woman, than any daughter. *My daughter is frightened and feels alone*, quavered the mother's heart.

The ghost instantly existed in melancholy, unremitting until the next mood change, which came about at the first new word.

Up till Regina had climbed into the tub Ophelia had been a whirlwind of confusion herself, watery images and memory colliding unaligned, her ghost-self knowing only to hover near the blood-hum it instinctively knew. In the bathroom she knew who what when where, rudimentarily how, no clue why, and sweetly, like the experience of a cold drink from a lovely fountain, that the naked woman made of water was her daughter.

The first new word was "Dennis." Weak, the way Regina said it, almost letting water into her mouth with her head lolled so far to the side. She kept her eyes closed. Steam sidled into her nostrils.

The mood of the ghost's universe became hopeful.

When Dennis crossed the bathroom threshold Regina's bottom lip crimped. When his hand entered the water to touch and stroke her neck, she cried uncontrollably, knowing instinctively that she had not truly spoken with her dead mother.

"In the simplest terms," said Skillet the next morning, "your house has issues."

Reverend Daville peered from under his thick eyebrows at Skillet, then at Regina and Dennis.

Empty words. Meaningless and, as Daville's attention returned to Skillet, ill-fitting coming from that man's mouth.

Even Regina was wondering what idiot talk show he'd seen, but Skillet rolled over this unintentional anachronism. "Your mother," he explained, "died in shame."

"Mr. Dumas," Reverend Daville softly interjected.

"Only time you get a haunting is when a person dies in shame," said Skillet, which both men full well knew, "and don't pretend there are no ghosts—"

"There are no ghosts," Dennis said.

"There's us. Sometimes there's still us. There's more ghosts than living," Skillet said. "Got nothin' to do with movies and spook stories." He touched the back of Regina's hand on the tabletop, her other hand curled in her lap. "You walked into your mama, girl. Nothin' wrong with you."

She looked at him. Did this mean he visibly saw her sanity, did he see the worth of sanity in a modern world? She raised her chin to meet his gentle eyes. She felt very small. A triad of men in her kitchen watched over her, called together by herself, and each's message was tuned to perfection:

"You're OK, Regina."

"Baby, you're fine, you're fine."

"You just walked inside your mama."

That's all?

"Mr. Dumas." Reverend Daville again, thinking to suggest, "It might be better if she came to my office to talk."

Regina swung her head toward him, frowning. "You know, we haven't had a real chance to talk since I came home."

Skillet said to Dennis, "How's a man to talk about the spirit of Jesus and deny that same grace to Jesus' own? Opie asked for more than that, Ben Daville. Up in that church for too many years for you to practice sleights with her daughter."

"She doesn't need this just this minute, Web."

"What's she waitin' for?"

"Reverend Daville, does the church acknowledge ghosts?" Dennis asked flatly, in his mind filing whatever Reverend Daville was about to say as Point A.

"Yes."

"Regina, do you think you were, what, what," he looked to Skillet, "sharing space with your ma's spirit?" He couldn't bring himself to use the word *ghost* again as part of an adult conversation.

"I don't know what happened," she answered truthfully. Point B.

Last night she'd wanted all the lights except for those in the bedroom to remain on. They'd slept with the bedroom door closed. Just sensing that much light out there was enough to keep Dennis wide awake all night.

However, this morning she'd wanted no light, especially not during this kitchen convening, the four in the cool natural light of a gray sun seeming to yawn through the clouds. Reverend Daville listened. Skillet explained. Dennis rationalized to himself. Regina considered her new stature of being small and full of wonders.

"I think a doctor might be best," the reverend said.

"I'm not sick." Big thick bathrobe. Big warm slippers. Sweatpants. Sweatshirt.

"Toward the possibility that perhaps you blacked out yesterday." To Dennis: "In a panic you likely overlooked her. There're too many explanations for this to be talking about Ophelia Nevills' ghost," Daville said, his face apologetic toward Regina.

"Benjamin." Skillet was patient.

"Web, this woman was laid to rest."

"Her soul with God," Regina recited. "Her spirit eternal in each remembrance."

"Yes," said Daville.

"Where was I yesterday, then?"

"With God," Skillet said. "God is memory, Gina."

"I didn't see any tracks leading to the door. I was not with God, I was in the basement, and she and I both heard the doorbell ring," said Dennis.

Looking at them curiously Skillet asked, "What do you two *want* to have happened yesterday?"

"I didn't want this to happen," Regina said.

And Dennis, picturing the porch, just shook his head.

"Wiring," Reverend Daville said. "No matter the interpretation we shouldn't neglect that you need to see a doctor."

"I caught a chill yesterday. I don't feel sick."

"You called us over here," he reminded her. "You also don't remember Dennis running the house calling your name. No cause for alarm in that by itself but to suppose your mother's influence concerns me a bit."

Dennis said, "But the church acknowledges."

"Under extreme conditions only."

"Go to a doctor," Skillet said, squeezing her hand, "then sit down and talk with the Rev." He pushed away from the table. "I'ma run across the street if Charles still got his tools, check on this wiring. Ya'll eat yet?"

"No," answered Dennis.

"Fix her breakfast."

Reverend Daville's office was deliberate, meticulous, and surprisingly comforting. Regina hoped not to behave as though fascinated to be there. A real preacher man's den. She looked around for bits of connection between holy and human, heartened to see a photo of Valerie with husband and child on the mantle behind his desk, as well as the jar of tiny foil-wrapped chocolates by his multi-line phone. Two bibles, one facing him, the other whomever he counseled, were both opened on the desk; for the counseled to Genesis: "I like troubled folks to keep in mind that all things have a beginning before they start blaming others for their misfortunes." His own to wherever he'd left off the day before.

She twisted in her seat to better observe him at the coffee maker, catching him sniffing at the pot and scowling. He explained as he poured its contents out. "Melody always gets here before me and makes her coffee double strength. I'm too old to condone daily waste. Pah! Splashed the sweater. Is it warm enough in here for you?"

She nodded. She resumed her assay. The office was done in browns and rugs, oval throw rugs judiciously placed atop an old, faded carpet. On the walls: more family pictures, a few framed documents in Latin placed above eye level, an enlarged photograph taken at dusk of the sun setting behind forest hills. He had a large circular mirror and three rows of wall-mounted bookshelves that immediately drew her eye. Books on theology, divinity, mythology, cinematography, psychology, sociology, paleontology, mysticism, poetic interpretation and a four volume retelling of the Arthurian legend.

What was it Skillet had told her after Ma's funeral about having time to think? For him it had been a luxury, one he would have loved to have hunted down for himself. For Daville it seemed given, and that didn't seem fair.

"Inconsiderate of her to waste so much unless she plans to drink the whole pot," Daville complained, loud enough to turn Regina toward him again. "Two whole packages for one crucial cup of acid, one cup from a whole pot."

"She doesn't listen to you?"

"She's a biddy."

"So she doesn't listen to anybody."

"Exactly."

"There aren't any crosses in here, Reverend," she said, opting for comfort in boldface.

He acknowledged genially. "Jesus shouldn't suffer everywhere." He handed her the cup of hot water and a tea bag before returning to the coffee machine to rifle for sugar packets. "He and I are friends in this office; this is where He's always welcome to sit and chat with me, or I Him. His days, I suspect, are usually longer."

He took a sip of his own tea before crossing the room to take a seat. "Have you visited your mother recently?" he said as though Ma weren't dead but simply in a rest home.

"No, not recently."

"I walk the grounds when the weather permits. Don't stop, though, just walk through and around, thinking of them."

"I was out toward the end of summer."

"And wondering why are you here?" He said the words in comforting fashion, which caught her off guard.

"That's what you're thinking." He smiled. "Why am I here when I could be at work or in the supermarket and is this going to be long? People don't bless the mundane as they should. It is often a life saver."

He leaned forward, fingertips splayed along the bottom of his bible. "I hate sitting behind this desk," he said. "This office is for the most sincere of conversations; instead, I'm given this token of artificial authority. Anyone can sit behind a desk. You saw a doctor?"

"I've made an appointment. I feel fine, Reverend."

He still leaned forward, in wait. "I know. If Web wasn't concerned I knew not to be. However," he said and sat back, "I recall you as an inquisitive child."

Regina blew into her tea. Childhood was a ways off.

"Your mother and I often enjoyed talking."

"I remember."

"She could talk!" And again, with those raised eyebrows: "There's no reason you should assume I'm not available for the same with you."

"I've been—"

"Busy living."

She looked sardonically off to one side. "Why do I always feel like a little girl around you and Mr. Dumas?"

"Because you're a modern woman."

"I'm knocking at forty."

"Years. Melody is eighty but has the consideration of a teenager. I'm more interested in who you are, not the age you've reached. In what you want or need. You wear a cross," he said, lifting a finger to the tiny crucifix attached to a thin silver chain.

She wore it out of rote, a gift from someone long ago.

"The number who wear one who've never attempted more than two minutes consecutive thought to God or Heaven? Or been inside a church for any kind of direction? I will tell anyone who'll listen not to think of that cross as symbol but as compass. Have you been happy since the move?"

"I think so."

"Before the move?"

"I don't know. Happy."

"Happy. You haven't forgotten happiness? In that big city, weren't you trying to be happy?"

Ganos, Opply and Dawn rolled through her head. *How may I direct your call?*

One moment, please.

Please, one--one mo--just a—

One fucking moment to myself, if you goddamn please! Jesus!

"Getting home was accomplishment enough," said Regina.

"You didn't move here to get through the day, or get married. Or even begin to date your husband. Not for just enough."

He watched her drink her tea.

"Not to get through the day," he said.

Then he took his own sip.

"There's been no one to talk to about your mother," he offered.

Regina kept her head bowed to the cup in both hands, hating feeling easily read. *My aunts? The people who kept Ma on her feet? Need I remind you?*

And, God, I can't stand Valerie's husband!

"What should I say?" she finally asked. "Am I supposed to be on some quest to find my mother?"

"Nonsense. You knew your mother. Everything you say, do, breathe or feel, that's her. That's the Lord's gift. That's how you come to know God."

"I've never been a faithful churchgoer."

"Ophelia said as much. I don't dream to preach you into the front row by Sunday. How've you been emotionally since last week?"

"Drained. Silly. Wondering what I wanted to ask you. I feel more silly than anything else."

"Mourning can be impractical." He tapped his desk as though directing her to lay something crucial right there in front of him. "Have you formed a conclusion about the incident?"

"Reverend—"

"You know, this is the first time you've come to see me."

"Yes. Reverend," she said, and then paused with her mouth still open before snapping it shut and instead shifting her seating.

"Ophelia confided in me that you two weren't close. At this stage of your life certain questions have probably grown immense. Yes?"

"I don't know."

"I hate those words. Three easiest words. You've likely got monstrous questions. At your age, mine were. Valerie's are. It's all right. No one is ever where they're supposed to be. Your husband, Dennis, is a maelstrom, which," he said with a softening, "is to say he's a man of privacies."

"Of deep conviction."

"You know when a question or concern isn't addressed it doesn't go away."

"I worried myself into a ghost story?"

"Worried is the wrong sense. You know something happened, but don't know why. Without why, you can't really know what happened. I honestly don't feel there's need for concern. It was simple stress relief. The severity would seem disturbing—"

"She ever ask about her soul?" she interrupted.

When they were eleven Jonathan Hammer said white people hadn't received proper souls. His grandma had told him so. The few good ones were trying to get souls; rest were just being themselves.

Regina punched him really hard.

"She wasn't very religious at home, Reverend."

"She was faithful to her own beliefs. There were a few times she came to this office for spiritual advice. She couldn't hide guilt well at all. Actually," he said, easing deeper into his chair, "most of the time we talked about you. I doubt she ever got used to the word 'mother' in the context of her life."

"What was she asking for, then?" *Why so much trouble to have me?* "I thank her but if her path meant to take her elsewhere, so be it. I wouldn't begrudge her. Whatever children I never have had better understand the same of me."

"You've discussed children?"

"Vaguely."

"Grandmother, now, would've suited her perfectly."

What about the things I don't know! she shouted inwardly. Minutiae. Who befriended her? Who'd she dial on lonely days? Did she ever flirt with Charles Hutchfield or date anyone? No one at the funeral had stepped forward to say, *Hello. Your mother was wonderful. I treasure the time we spent shopping yard sales for porcelain dolls, the time we made ice cream, the way she dropped her eyes when she smiled. She would rub my neck sometimes without my asking.* Would he have been white or black, Asian—

Or even a woman?

Ma, these things happen. There're all kinds of twists and turns to an ordinary life.

"The worst part living here is that after a year I still have no idea who misses my mother. It follows me out the door every day. Who's missing her and waiting to see me so they can reach out? She didn't die; she was swallowed when everybody's head was turned."

To answer her, Daville said toward his bible, "I miss her."

She muttered "Hm?" not because she hadn't heard but because she wanted to hear it again.

"I miss her. Tell me something. What is it about life that hurts so, dear?"

"Do things seem pleasant for me?"

"Yes."

Where does the problem arise?

"They're not pleasant for everyone, Reverend."

"And?"

As I waste time dying I smile in remembrance of the time a baby monkey waved and Mama threw it a caramel against zoo rules. These thoughts unbidden come and I will not push them aside. As I waste time dying I taste the sudden lemon rush of my first perfectly achieved orgasm by my own trembling hand. I see a succession of intrinsic moments.

It is a fool who wants something out of life.

"And?" Daville prodded.

Regina smiled. "I feel foolish."

"No episodes since?" he asked just to be sure, relieved when she shook her head. Young people were so easily psychotic these days. "But you do still suspect it was Ophelia?" he said, again to be sure.

"Haven't you ever seen Jesus during your talks?" she said, before adding, "If you don't mind my asking."

He scratched his forehead simply for the pleasurable distraction of it. He peered at her with what Web called "weight" so that she wouldn't get the impression he was a foolish old man, desk or no desk.

"I've felt him."

"I've seen my mother."

"You've remembered her. The grieving process is especially tricky sometimes."

Church matron Melody sidled past the open office door. "Grieving? Impractical."

Regina half smiled.

"I want to talk with you!" Daville shouted. "I'm sorry."

"Reverend Daville, I don't expect you to transform Ma for me." She leaned forward herself. "I want to know one thing."

"Yes?"

"She never smiled much. She learned to, didn't she?"

"Yes."

Regina smiled. "Did she have a beautiful smile?"

"Yes."

Boot. Snow. Hole.

Boot. Snow. Hole. Crunching through a frosty cereal bowl. Below freezing temperatures had changed the top of the snow into a cracker.

In her mind Regina was massive. Prehistoric wearing neoprene shoes. She was two people: the one whose warm boots met brittle resistance from what was supposed to be yielding snow, and, instantly, the one the snow couldn't hope to resist.

Absolutely prehistoric.

Her breath puffed with the exertion of having to raise her legs so high. Looking ahead, the wintry vista presented the delirious and glorious mood of being not the last but the only person on earth. The only woman for the world to choose from. Her cold cheeks pulled into a smile behind the scarf. Wild Woman with staunch sidekick, Ghost Mom!

"There're certain things religious folk simply are incapable of understanding," Regina mumbled. "Like souls. How they never go away."

But she had no mind now to think about souls. Mama had decided to have a child; her child decided to be born. That was enough.

Since it was cold out, the fun of walking home through the snow would wear out in another three or four blocks. Those blocks were not yet walked. For now, with scarf and cap and gloves and boots and morning quietude courtesy of folks not so constitutional, she was happy knowing that home awaited. Somehow—no, she knew how—Reverend Daville's assurance left her with the distinct sense that the answer to all questions about her dead mother was that her mother was dead, taken to God, but in memory Ophelia rises like a mood, from darkness to brightest light, from death to the terrible reaffirmation, that of life. One lived.

One living.

When she got home there was the sense that all answers to questions about the dead are that the dead are dead, just as the living are living. "Memory brings us to where we are. When Reverend Daville said *that*, it was like a tuning fork dinging a bell," she told Dennis.

"You're still going to the doctor."

"Yes."

But I am no longer afraid, and if the winter kills me I will return in the spring, slash its throat sweetly, and whistle a pretty tune. I will feel no shame.

Thalia watched the world sleep, quietly musing on what subtle dreams to weave into that which was, is, and will be of human history, not because she cared one way or another but because it was wasteful not to take advantage of sleeping things.

9

The New World

George Sumner decided on the small coastal city of Dorset, county of Webster, for his equally small but effective counterstrike. *Lois Lanes*, for those who wish to be saved. Computers, amazing machines. Full of angels. All it took was Dorsett demonstrating how to use the geo-search while her father peered closely at her fingers on the keyboard. On a whim she used her own name as a search point, narrowing one hundred and forty-seven locales to fifteen using the criteria he rattled off to her. Finally he picked Regina's hometown because it was near water, and water was peace. Dorset, county of Webster, was small enough for people to know one another yet large enough for them to fear each other.

Racially diverse. Twelve percent unemployment rate, which meant they were used to crime. Had been the site of a notoriously inept Klan rally decades ago; not easy to instill sufficient fear to force the savages home when half your conspirators are dashing for the bushes from doctored soda.

Black folks actually laughed them out of town.

And the inhabitants of Dorset were Americans. America and violence were synonymous.

Sumner nodded and clucked his tongue. *For you, Lois.* They needed saving.

"Why not purchase land now to have the park built by spring?" suggested Dorsett.

"Are they buried under snow there?"

"Probably."

Sumner's eyes brightened considerably. "Buy the land! Put a big sign up: 'Future site of...' but don't tell them what." He pushed away from the workstation and stood painfully, saying, "Then phone whichever of my lawyers and foist the unimportant bits off."

By springtime Robert Michilane, precisely because he didn't try, only because he didn't try, had gained enough points with Norton that catching fish with this nutty white guy probably wasn't as ludicrous as it sounded.

The sun was wet and warm. After a paltry winter, fish bit at anything. Norton kept on pretending to know how to bait a hook. His innate assessment was that it didn't *feel* ludicrous. As long as Robert kept to himself and didn't try to get under Norton's skin, Norton didn't have a problem saying fuck you to Penny Ante and all the other wasted fiends. They were still his source of money but not a one would be missed if they were gone.

Shaffer had come, though. He was the one purchased the fishing gear. Got it from a second hand shop, three rods, three reels, nicked, rusted, deities forbid a fish show gumption against the reel Norton used. First sign of trouble its gears would cocoon into a tangled mass of five-pound test. Norton hadn't known Shaffer was coming. Turned out it didn't matter; Shaffer kept to himself, too.

Norton kept watch on them when his bobber had nothing to do. Robert was crazy but he always acted like he had things on his mind. Sweetheart had a thing for the spaz but he acted like he didn't have a dick to be affected by things like a man should.

Sometimes it was like both men were spies who'd have to kill anybody catching them revealing the truth.

Spaz didn't talk much, either. In the car, Norton's attention had lapsed for a moment and he missed all of Shaffer's small talk.

Robert approached along the gravel bank.

"Biting for you, Air Force?"

"It's quiet," Norton said.

Robert plopped his rump on the ground and rummaged through the makeshift tackle box. "You are not fishing," he had defined prior for Shaffer's benefit, "without a tackle box. No tackle box is standing around pissing in the water."

"Might attract a big one that way," Shaffer'd joked.

Norton glanced down the bank at Shaffer. Shaffer's rod was propped in the crotch of a forked stick driven into the ground.

"He's looking for rocks again," Norton informed Robert.

"I know. That's why we're about to go tightline." The older men had gotten into a game of throwing stones toward the other's spots whenever one of them caught a fish. Norton had heard a huge laugh the first time and looked up surprised to see Shaffer as the source.

Norton didn't know much about fishing but knew throwing rocks in the water couldn't be the most efficient means toward a huge catch.

Unless fish were extremely stupid.

Norton decided they must be, but didn't throw any rocks himself. Instead, cast by cast, he'd moved farther along the bank until eventually a good twenty-five yards separated him from Robert, and ten more separated Robert from Shaffer. Norton came to fish, not play.

"What's tightline?" he asked.

"Man fishing." He'd told Shaffer to buy an assortment of teardrop-shaped lead weights. "Get rid of that bobber."

"Ain't that how you know you got a bite?"

"With man fishing you have to *feel* it. No old woman's bells, either. Either hold on to it or watch the tip of it. Very homoerotic." He dropped the rest of the contents back into the art-cum-tackle box and regained his feet, saying offhand, "You haven't gone down on a woman yet so you don't have that kind of patience." He walked off and tossed a weight toward Shaffer, who stopped reeling long enough to snatch the heavy teardrop from the air.

"You cast out farther going tightline," Robert shouted back.

Bigger fish, Norton realized. He didn't want to seem too eager. In a few minutes he'd go tightline.

Robert and Shaffer now fished closer together, their lines flying out great distances before dropping with sharp plops into the choppy water.

"You watch much TV, Shaffer?"

"Nope. Never have."

"You must've been a weird kid. I was on TV."

"Bullshit."

"That's what I thought. I was on a couple years ago. *Life's Work.*"

"Is that right?"

The water stretched a quarter mile to the opposite shore of their man-made parkland lake, a great ovoid fish trap complete with sediment, seaweed and mossy algae patches. Gravel lined the banks. Behind them, grass ran freely in every direction, dotted with saplings here and about. There was a wharf a little farther down past a filtration station. The water wasn't blue. Robert had been married the last time he saw clear blue water, an anniversary vacation to some tropical tourist enclave, replete with store-bought safety. This water was cloudy gray even though the spring sky was blue, was clear, was as wide as the space behind his eyes.

Shaffer paid Robert no attention. He was trying to remember if his father had ever actually taught him anything about fishing or had he as a child learned by osmosis.

Sirens raced up and down Dorset's paved streets behind them. A lost boy had been found without actually being found, because no one knew he was lost. Or had known. It was Ralph, but no one yet knew that either. He'd been fished out of other waters, half-naked, bloated to decomposition, but with half a broom handle still stuck up his ass and a single bullet hole at the very top of his head, his soul peering helplessly out of that hole, crying profusely, refusing to leave the cold cramped confines of that body, not even under the glare of television cameras or the scrutiny of the medical examiner, or the detectives assigned to his case whose scrotums constricted whenever they thought of that broom handle. If he cried and flailed long enough, the body might awaken from shame alone. Gray rotted linking of flesh! Traitor!

The natural eloquence of souls revealed itself.

I am betrayed!

Please don't tell anyone I am dead, it should have been said. By God if no one else. *This has not happened!*

He peered, face pressed to the cranium, hands crammed against the interior of the skull, hearing the laughter the living laughed by dint of being alive.

Somewhere I have a friend, he knew.

But could not remember who.

"I ain't catch nothin' tightline," Norton told Sweetheart, who was aggressively packing four small fish in the small freezer compartment of her refrigerator.

"Where you sleepin' tonight?"

"Too early to think about it."

"Boy, it's after dark. Think." She rammed the last fish as far as she could.

"You gon' let me stay here?" he said hopefully but noncommittally.

Her hands were cold. She wanted to warm them around his throat.

Norton watched her guardedly. Her jaw was set too tight for her to be buzzed, unless she'd been hitting mad weed.

She marched past without speaking to him but muttered loud enough for him to deal with, "You're not my goddamn son," then went into the bathroom and closed the door to wash her hands of fish.

When she crawled into bed after midnight she wondered if he was somewhere asleep too.

Spring was not her favorite time of the year because the consensus of thought was on beauty, and she was not beautiful.

The moment she awoke she threw a robe on and crossed the hall to Shaffer's door.

He answered it fully dressed and appeared instantly irritated with her.

"Why you ain't tell me you were goin' fishing with him?"

He closed the door behind him, edging her to the middle of the hall.

"It's Sunday. I'm on my way to church."

"I can be brief. How well you know the boy?"

"He hangs around the store with Robert—"

"The hot dog?"

"Often as you've been hanging around the store yourself, you know."

"But I see he around you when I ain't."

"It's too sad for me to think about."

"Me too. You seen the news?"

"No."

"Then buy a newspaper when you come outta church." She turned back to her apartment, leaving him standing there in his sweats and jacket.

Church was Dorset's meager art museum, which had somehow gotten hold of a series of J. P. Miller paintings. Sweetheart had almost made him forget his sketch pad.

Mythic heroes were so much better to sketch because they were like comic heroes only more real. Miller's *Fall* series consisted of four paintings, black and red with smudges of white for tone and highlight, of mythic figures in portraits aflame, the figures' own bodies trailing red smoke into the blackened backgrounds. *Hercules*, face slightly downcast, eyes obscured in deep shadow, appeared ashamed of the power in one opened hand, bright red with inherent flame, and the other a cool, embered fist, a thing of granite regardless of whether he wished to yield. His barrel chest strode parted the flames, his heart not in war.

Bolo-Dai, Chinese hero of the *Seventeen Dragons*, entrusted to serve and protect each dragon but fully aware all seventeen were the cause of his family's misfortunes. He burned brighter than the flames, as if he'd fed on each dragon's heart, the dragons barely discernible sewn into the patterns of the swirling smoke.

Lomo of the Sudan, the succubus ordered by all Natural Gods to give birth as punishment for her crimes against patience, ordered to give birth and to love the child, a male child, never to know of his godlike lineage.

Finally, *Merlin*. Hawkish, bony face creased in worry, face turned just slightly in a sideways glance, the black smoke thick on all sides and wrapping around to tap at the space where—had he been human—his heart would have been. But Miller's Merlin was more incantation than man, a spectral figure in human shape, the sword Excalibur held impotently in his lap. He had no heart. What worried the world's one true sorcerer? Miller had titled this painting, "The Coming of the King?"

Shaffer's pencils whizzed over his paper, sketching the fierily baroque curves of Lomo's fatal body, the succubus' hairless African sex emerging through smoke with the intent of stepping off the canvas in one final enduring act of rebellious seduction.

Greece, China, Africa, Europe. No matter where, heroism meant raging against one's own nature. He identified with this because—as he drew Lomo, the progenitor of all rueful souls—he thought forcibly of Sweetheart, who in his mind was actually Regina. He ripped Sweet Regina's clothes off the way women favored it, yanking the blouse downward just enough to free the shoulders, then lower, pinning the arms with her own fabric, exposing her bosom jutting proud and defiant under the shameful spell of her own arousal.

His erection was safely tucked under the jacket in his lap. Besides, he shared these religious experiences with no one. This early on a Sunday he was practically alone in the museum, have mercy.

He prayed there was a spot on his neck she'd find. It was one Phaedra Mason had accidentally brushed lifting her reassuring hand from his shoulder two days before the end of the semester, which was three days before making tentative love to him in her basement studio.

He'd let it happen because even though she was rather plump what she was doing to him felt rather good. Her professorial ministrations even gave him time to construct a brief ode to the experience. Her hands kneaded his buttocks like clay. Making love with her was not so much a seduction as it was an exercise in experiencing a mood, succumbing to it, discarding it, then moving on in favor of the next. She asked what things felt like, not licentiously but curiously. "Have you been blown by an older woman?" she asked, squishing his buttocks, pulling the head of his penis closer to her downy face. He didn't answer immediately because he felt ridiculous with his pants and underwear bunched around the tops of his ankles and tennis shoes. *My feet are huge*, he thought.

The way his fantasies invariably ran these days, Regina Nevills, through a series of erotic discoveries, unerringly found the neck spot and fell upon it with delicious swirling motions, the immediate pleasure thereby elevating the reverie from *concurrent* consciousness to *the* conscious, making him have to do three things: shake it off, rethink his position in the scheme of things, and reapply pencil to paper with pointed vigor.

He stopped a moment, flipped backward to Hercules and Bolo-Dai, both of which had been completed last week, and briefly studied the strokes of his hand, regaining appreciation for the paths and pressures he was capable of creating. He re-flipped to Lomo, her arms raised in a sympathetic mixture of defiant beseeching that drew her muscled bosom taut. He decided on a challenge: finish her in fifteen minutes flat.

The tragedy of heroism, he thought. *Rushed art.* Fantasies faded as his mind became a function of his hand again.

Sweetheart was there again that afternoon, following him from the glass-littered entry of the apartment complex, ending up at his door, giving off airs of urgency that irked and intrigued him. Without thinking on the precise moment of her change, he knew she *had* changed. Over the course of the past few months he'd had three occasions of almost thinking to invite her in.

All the way to the apartment she kept asking about the fishing trip. Whose idea it'd been, where'd they go, why hadn't he told her anything about it?

"Why're you goin' fishin' with him but he can't keep the fish in your freezer?"

"Does he live with me? Will you go away?"

He unlocked his door and entered with her smoothly entering behind him. He tossed his keys and sketchpad on the sofa. In the crook of his arm was a newspaper that he dropped aside, purposely keeping his back to her.

"I worry about him. Did you read it?"

"No," he said.

"Found a boy yesterday with a broomstick up his ass. Been missing for months. Wasn't dead for months."

This stopped him short. Still with his back to her: "How old?"

"Fifteen."

He was relieved that it hadn't been a small child.

"Bullet to the head."

"Running with the wrong crowd," he said. He faced her.

She hadn't moved from beside the door.

"Gangs don't fuck boys up the ass."

No possible riposte to a statement like that. Shaffer kept quiet.

Sweetheart appeared as though were it possible for her to cry, she was small enough not to take up too much room if he needed to console her.

"What's this got to do with me and Robert? Did Norton know the boy?"

"Nobody knows the boy."

"Just like nobody knows Norton."

She nodded. "Been in the water too long."

"I'm not his mentor, and he doesn't think of me as a friend," said Shaffer. Furthermore, Shaffer didn't even like Norton.

"Can you watch out for him, though, if I can't? It's not like I'm asking you something big."

In a month Norton went missing too.

10

Violence

"If you see him let me know," said Regina.

"How's things going with you and Dennis?" asked Mrs. Hutchfield.

"Wonderful."

"What happened to him, baby?"

"A friend's looking for him."

Mrs. Hutchfield studied the photocopied sketch of Norton. "Boy too young for so hard a face. A stray, isn't he?"

"I don't like that word," said Regina.

"Neither do I."

Leanna, Regina was certain, saw clear around the world from her porch.

Because another child had disappeared within that same month, another boy, reports skewed toward the possibility of gangs, Satanists, sexual predators, and a combination thereof. Someone wanted boys. No one had yet come forth to claim the first young Doe, the boy whom people still prayed for. *Dear God*, they prayed, *Help us.*

Everyone who thought of him felt stripped below the waist, sodomized, then still and numb, brains observing a moment of silence.

Springtime brought no beauty.

Regina numbly drove past a sizable plot of land under development, its fencing flypapered with notices of danger and future grandeur. She knew what it was. Everyone knew what it was. Land had been cleared, then dirt brought in for landscaping, little man-made hillocks with squares of grass being laid out like rows of dominoes around massive holes.

Something rich wanted something built over the grave of a large, defunct department store situated near downtown Dorset a few blocks off the main avenue.

She gave no thought to it. A ghost in the form of twenty sketches rode the car seat beside her, some boy she'd never seen, contained now in a blue plastic folder she'd pilfered a long time ago from Ganos, Opply and Dawn.

She'd called in sick to help Shaffer distribute the notices, and was on her way to Valerie. Valerie would certainly know where strays wound up.

She entered the nondescript municipal building, received her badge from Big Chris-at-the-supermarket's security officer cousin, and listened to him tell her she was looking a little tired—

"Seen better days, Wade."

Like Big Chris, Wade harbored a crush on her. It helped to pass the time.

On impulse she handed him one of the sketches. "If you see this boy let me know." She wrote her phone number above that of Sweetheart's.

"He's a runner." He answered her frown by saying, "You wouldn't be here if you didn't think so."

She smiled sadly. It would probably be inappropriate to pat him on the side of the face. "I'm helping somebody else."

"Then somebody knew what he was involved with. I work private surveillance evenings. I run across anything—" he said and let it hang.

Dorset's Chief Probation Officer never let her office appear inactive. Files were everywhere, neatly everywhere, but nonetheless everywhere. Her phone never stopped ringing.

Not until seeing the complexity of this operation did Regina gain an appreciation for how great a percentage of the human race was on probation.

No family pictures in her office, explained, she'd said, as prudent precaution. Occasionally she conducted interviews in this office. Last thing she needed was someone with a grudge biding their time until they recognized somebody from the picture out in the park or coming out some door. "People on probation are the most bitter, misbegotten excuses you'll never want to know. Fault whoever they see behind a desk for life itself, get released, then go back to the street with the God-given right to screw up."

She was rolling a new pair of stockings on under her desk when Regina entered.

Regina waved and sat wearily. She hadn't started the week wearily, but Shaffer's call had instantly set weariness in motion.

"Without a door your office is a glorified cubicle," she observed dryly.

"Nobody can see anything." Discretely, Valerie raised her hips to bring the crotch home. "I hate these."

Regina picked at a frayed spot on the seam of her jeans.

"You look like shit," Valerie noted.

Regina passed a flyer to her.

"You're a good one for helping. He doesn't look familiar," said Valerie.

"It's hard carrying these around. I don't even know him. Where do they go?"

"Kids who hang around dope houses?"

"I don't know that he did."

"They go mostly back to the dope houses."

"Gamebirds flying with vultures."

"Basically."

"No way this boy's going to be found is there?" asked Regina.

Valerie wanted to offer a semblance of encouragement. The simplest thing she could say was, "At least we're looking. I'll post this."

The only hope was whomever had him didn't have a broom handy.

Would've been monstrous to say so aloud.

"Not impossible, is it?" Regina wondered.

Valerie directed a silent prayer toward the sketch while saying, "You got time to eat?"

"I've got time."

"I'll buy."

"You seen him yet?" Robert asked Shaffer.

"This ain't my search, Robert. I did the sketch."

"Didn't know she wasn't his mother."

"Now she wants to be."

"He have a real mother?"

"Apparently not."

"Got his guidance from people with their heads up their collective ass."

"And you didn't?"

"Watch yourself."

Sweetheart tracked Penny to his latest squat, a staid bungalow a few blocks from his last, with that same old dog that for unknown reasons had attached its future to his travels. No one had ever seen Penny feed it.

Brown Ass Dog was scruffy but not ugly. It backed automatically from the human encroachment of Sweetheart passing the front steps toward the backyard, where she gave the knock to gain entry.

The boy who answered looked about eighteen. Penny didn't want folks thinking he had a thing for little boys and brooms, not when word had already filtered among the dealers that two of his had come up missing. Enough people knew the boy fished ass up out of the water had to be Ralph, and if Sweetheart was looking for Norton all eyes swiveled round to Penny again.

She nudged past the boy, knowing Penny was somewhere ahead pretending to be lord of an empire.

The boy grabbed her arm. "You buyin' this time? Why don't you suck my dick?" he said, managing to sound genuinely curious as to why it wasn't a given.

She shrugged away, saying, "Need tweezers for your ugly ass," and kept walking. "Where he at?"

"Gettin' fucked for the rock," Gene said, grinning stupidly the way teenaged boys grin. He kept his hands in the pockets of his loose fitting pants to let her know his hands weren't far from his gun.

"Charlene again?"

Still that stupid grin. "He loves him some Charlene."

"He'd love you if you bent over far enough."

Gene drew up.

Sweetheart listened. Dope fiends were so numb you'd never get a peep even with a pneumatic fuck. A man'd get more moans out of a date with his soaped up hand.

But now she discerned the tight, urgent creakings of a bed.

Most dealers allowed about three handpicked regulars to build up healthy credit ratings in exchange for personal relations.

Most dealers were ugly as sin; that certain women became walking lotion tended to build confidence for Rial Pendle beyond his wildest dreams. Sweetheart had been one. All her sleeping dreams were reenactments of the year she'd put out enough poon every man in Dorset should've gotten a contact high.

Then a grunt, Penny's, like somebody had surprised him with a smack across the ass and he wanted to stifle the pain. She pictured him coming with his eyes open the way dealers always did with relations, eyes open and looking at some piece of furniture or at the spot just above the woman's head.

A second later Charlene emerged, her small bag of drugs protected deep in her pocket, looking at no one and nothing but somehow aware this was the way to the door. Naturally she was small and thin. Under no circumstances should anyone allow her to smile.

For a short time Sweetheart and Charlene had worked as a tandem. Penny got to watch Charlene tongue Sweetheart when he was just the lookout in somebody else's squat.

Today, Charlene didn't exist. Sweetheart barely saw her as the thin sandblasted woman smudged past; yet even Charlene ignored Gene despite how his body language and position in her path were trying to interest her in confidence building exercises for himself.

God, he was stupid!

Didn't he know a fiend got no use for dick? Might as well use a broomst—

Her stomach fell.

Penny emerged right behind Charlene, and stopped short.

"I ain't seen him."

"Nobody you work with seen him?"

"My dick is still wet."

"I'm sure you spend plenty time with it dry."

"Get up in here." He pulled her quickly into the bedroom and closed the door. The mattress' disheveled top covers meant nothing to her. There was nothing else in the room except a ratty yellow chair and the light switch on the wall.

"Why all of a sudden you tryin' to be real?" Rial asked. "Remember yourself."

"Nobody you work with seen him?"

"No."

They squared off on each other.

"Don't bring no police 'round me," Rial said.

"Motherfucker, I know too many people to consider anything *you* say a threat. He better not turn up like Ralph, Penny."

Penny threw his hands up. "Ralph fucked up somewhere! Nothin' to do with me! Norton wasn't but on the fringes. Hell, bitch, you know them boys are Kleenex."

"This is the flyer," she said, her arm out for him to take it.

He made her wait, then took it, unfolded it, and admitted it looked damn like Norton, little dog-killing fool. "*Don't bring no police 'round me*," he reiterated.

"I don't hear nothin' about him in seven days I'ma damn sure mention you to somebody."

"Girl, it ain't like he just worked for me!"

"Nobody else is as bitch-assed as you, and you the one he was with the most."

"I put him out."

196

"And you took him right back. You better find me out something in seven days."

"I don't know what you think's protectin' you from a bullet up your ass--"

She opened the bedroom door wide. "I know the size of your dick," she said, then couldn't help a dopey grin herself. "Mama told me not to sweat the small stuff."

———————————————

———————————————

It happened like this: Norton, walking well after dark, just happened to think he'd seen a naked woman dance past some blinds she probably thought were fully closed. Or she thought no one could see her with such a dim source of lighting in the living room as the television. He backed up and waited.

There she was again.

He made sure the streets were deserted and crept closer. She danced like a white girl, all hand motions and hip twists.

But she was naked—mostly naked—and he was fourteen.

By the time he got close enough to her window, careful to avoid trampling her plants, he was peering unfettered through the blind's slats at the back of her neck and shoulder blade where a mid-calf kimono had slipped. The kimono was open, its sash hanging limp like someone forced to slow dance.

For a moment she stood in sharp relief. She picked something up, no longer dancing. Just moving around the room now. Naked in her home as though no one had eyes at night.

Frequently she went out of view. Finally she sat in the chair across from the TV. Bluish lights strobed as she flipped channels. Her kimono was wide open.

Norton moved to the window's bottom left corner and strained his eyes to see. Most of her was in shadow. She leaned forward, bored that nothing was on TV, just as a commercial flared brightly. In that clear view of her, Norton realized there was a God.

Her elbows were on her knees. Breasts dangled. Darkness obscured her nipples, but he knew nipples were there.

For the next thirty seconds she did nothing but plant her chin in her palm and gaze at the floor. She had pretty hair; it hung down naturally like a damn good perm. Norton looked at the car parked in front of her house. It looked like a woman's car. Maybe she lived alone.

Regina got up and stretched a stretch that carried her off the balls of her feet, giving him a good three-quarter view of her face, bosom, bush and legs.

Wildly, he imagined she knew he was there and was putting on a show for him.

God provides!

He found his calling. There was no harm in this, no junkies, no guns, theft, dogs, missing friends or more friends who might come up missing, no questions about life or purpose, and as long as he could get cereal out of Sweetheart, no need for profit. He felt as though he'd been missing out on naked people in the night his entire life.

His heart pounded whenever it seemed she might come close to the window and spot tiny glints of light, but he didn't move.

God provides.

She paid no attention to that window.

He felt a moment of hatred for her because she hadn't invited him inside.

He grew to love the idea of watching her every night, coming to love her awkward, unhurried movements, losing himself, dissolving Norton Fairchild away until there was no need to be Norton or anyone else, no need to be.

Simply to see.

His erection taught him Sanskrit. Conscious thought flowed with the blood to his young penile head. A truth, impossible for him to express yet, glistened within his pants as, without exaggeration, the end all and be all of human experience:

Voyeurism.

That's all there is, his penis told him, *There is no more.*

We lonely hunters hunt prey by seeing without being seen.

The predation blues.

Regina showed him the way and the means to paradise. Hell was a function of visibility. Heaven belonged to those who could render themselves invisible.

Mr. Bojangles, perched comfortably atop a telephone pole across the street, stood proudly erect.

It waited to be sure. Invisibility alone was not enough. To truly achieve, it was necessary to see the *invisible* things that danced and pranced as though they could not be seen. The girl who lived in the house in front of Norton's eyes had seen; that was why it continued to gravitate to her: she did the magic thing! She *saw* it, invisible little black girl looking at the invisible black night, looking for something which had failed to *see* her, faced only with the night and what the night was made of: stars, silence, gravity wells and mysteries.

It knew the concept of monkey; it knew the concept of roof, having pulled these from the girl's mind in order to context itself in relation to her.

She had been silly enough to think those other children owned monkeys.

Two invisible beings seen by each other see only the truth.

From his perch, Bojangles watched angels appear and disappear, popping in and out like gusts of snow melting on contact with air. It loved their incandescence; everything about them screamed of impermanence! The way they were ashes with the last dying hints of red flaring the edges.

When death had occurred in that house the angel of death hadn't appeared to recognize itself because, quite understandably—and Bojangles was somewhat chagrined not to have realized this—gods were dying elsewhere. They had more physical attraction, in the strict sense of physics, to the stream of Death's Angels' particles than the slowing blood hum of this girl's mother.

The upper echelon gods of Olympus finally died in the twenty-first century.

Even though the angels who comprised (they did not cause) death were many, they functioned as one in noting as many deaths as possible until such time as they came upon the one death that was death itself. In this way they functioned as foraging ants swarming over a forest floor, but were industrious, independent, wildly collective but unsure from which direction their queen issued her directives.

Even an angel knew it would sooner recognize itself in the death of a god than in Ophelia Nevills.

And if Ophelia hadn't been Regina's mother, Bojangles wouldn't have been interested in Ophelia either. The source of vision had come from both parents, though, and Bojangles had visited Regina's father often enough, drawn to the people Regina tended to wonder about.

And never just Regina. There were families whose entire genealogy it logged, entire communities that knew of it and it of them to the extent that at certain times humans might catch a glimpse of a spider-monkey out of the corner of their eyes.

The boy's primal thought continued its outward communication, that of a cat stroking against a leg, a poorly understood pleasure without complication.

But unlike Bojangles, this boy felt joy in the seeing precisely because he wasn't supposed to see, not because there was something that existed *to be seen*.

Bojangles perched no less proud.

Norton had seen bigger tits in magazines and porn, had even seen another fourteen-year-old take off her clothes, panties included, for him—but wouldn't allow more than a fingering—and had observed that her breasts looked like inverted teacups. To see a woman in an open kimono was on a different magnitude altogether.

He realized that for the two minutes he watched her she was his. Entirely. A woman who belonged to a fourteen-year-old boy. A woman could belong to a fourteen-year-old boy.

He hadn't been reading newspapers, nor had television become a source of information, so he didn't know the specifics of Ralph's predicament. He knew he was dead, had known a week or so after that Friday when Ralph failed to show up and the only thing Norton's inquiries brought forth was irritation at a fool boy's problems.

Norton was glad Regina didn't touch herself; it would've made him suspect she knew he was there.

But after he left when the television went out and she went to bed, he imagined plenty ways she might've pleasured herself. He cut through an unlit weedy vacant lot between two brick buildings that long ago had been boarding houses, and was grabbed by someone who, while Norton was watching *her*, happened upon that same moment to watch him, a huge hulking man whose mind had long ago slowed to glacial pacing to the point that he had become willy-nilly a force of nature.

"I bring you love," he whispered into Norton's ear, one thick hand over Norton's mouth forcing Norton to realize with a panic that despite the gun in his pants he was still a fourteen-year-old boy. Fingers clamped into his jawbones, not overly painful but more than an efficient deterrent: instead of trying to cry out, the boy was trying to struggle away, wasting energy, wasting the last bit of time... before... the... End.

In Valerie's bedroom, at 12:38 a.m., calm notions of dreams ripple the blue-black lake upon which stars skate. She sees Regina dive and decides to dive in too. The two Eves swim without communication. Each is a fish, arms arcing out gracefully in the night, sluicing peaceably back into the placid water. They are alert to the plips and plops their exertions make and focus on these small occasions intently, for small things are the sigils of life. Like dolphins, this plip means I am here, that plip means you are there, these plips mean we are near. The near passage of angling bodies is not marked so much as the noises they make.

The intrusive noise. The violence of inherent existence.

They swam through the Permian. Of course it was violent, things tried to eat them. But there was no malice. But nor was there love.

In the Triassic, something so huge it was simply a disembodied *mouth*, slick, wide open and full of teeth, shattered Valerie's ribcage but lost sight of her in the foam and spray. It struck again anyway, gorging on huge mouthfuls of water and aquatic vegetation. Fifty feet below, Valerie sank and continued to sink, a concave gash in her chest where once she'd had big bazooms, fish darting with their mouths open through the trail of chum her body left: the bits of intestine, pulps of bloody streamers, the regurgitated contents of her stomach even though she couldn't remember having eaten a full meal that day; she and Regina had nibbled on a few red nubbly berries and a heaping of cool fresh water but...

Sigh. Sweet and simple sigh. Breath for sighing. Her body, limp but for the currents—which she'd never suspected possessed their own differential strata—sank into darkness with the last of her air. She was in the place where fish had no eyes. Teeth came at her from all sides unseen. She began to feel put upon.

The friends evolved plating in the Cretaceous, which deadened their ability to feel or be felt. With the plating came the knowledge of tactical maneuvers.

These came in handy when the meteor obliterated the earth. They survived.

They swam a gauntlet of battles during Joan D'Arc's bloody reign as a priestess of Ra. Mix-ups abounded. Confusion terrified. Terror led to rage. Valerie gave as well as she got, beheading twenty men who looked surprisingly like Michael, Sr., she slipping naked from the water camouflaged and slick with muck, lightning in her eyes reflecting off the loud noises of war. Metal met bone and a new word was born: efficiency, need, lust, crave, worship. Malice. Malice before thought.

The efficiency of murder taught those about to die the truest appreciation of life: that they should have been the ones on the handle end.

Or the hilt, as the case may be.

It wasn't a time to think about Regina. Twenty more men first to be beheaded.

She dreamed she climbed atop her husband and, together, made a golden child. She slept through the night and in the morning awoke to Michael, Jr.'s cries.

"Hips and kisses can't lie," Valerie said around her mouthful of cod. "Women make bad liars because of that. Reggie?"

"Hm?"

"Where you at?"

The lemon-skinned woman with elfin eyes shrugged. Specifics were missing. Was she where she was supposed to be?

"You've been real heavy," said Valerie.

Regina poked her fish with the tines of her fork and asked, "Do you pray much?"

"Not enough. Prayer irks God. Don't tell Uncle Ben I said that." Valerie's phone buzzed. Michael. "He's forever looking for me when I'm at lunch." She dug into her purse. "You don't mind?" she asked.

"If you don't mind knowing how that tastes with fish," Regina said, then tuned Valerie out as Valerie left for whatever neutral spot she could find within the restaurant.

Dennis might want to take me dancing tonight, she decided. They'd never gone dancing.

He loved her so much he'd even love the fact that she couldn't dance.

But what about God? Sardonically, she prayed for God to go to hell and come back a changed deity, laying her hand on the blue folder of very likely a dead boy.

"I love you, Dennis." What was he cooking for dinner? A headache was beginning. She admonished herself for continuing to torture her food. Rows of tiny holes dotted the seared Tilapia's surface like tribal scars. *Wouldn't it be nice to have someone call me about my son?* she imagined.

To have that kind of connection between three people.

To be inseparably linked no matter how hard the child tried to break off and away. Like she'd pretended she had for longer than it was worth.

She'd grow old realizing that's simply what children did; they did meaningless things out of some internal need to be meaningful.

Besides, if she was lucky, her child might be the one:

(1) for whom the perspective *Children change everything;*

(2) to give life to the perspective *Children change everything;*

(3) for whom it would indeed be said, "Children change everything."

"Beloved, I hope you've known other ways," she'd write on a farewell card to him. A card Skillet might keep safe then deliver in the future when there was time to sit and think, time to judge whether immortality was a foregone waste. By the

time her son became a man all of Dorset might be a park. He and Skillet might sit inside a breeze and breathe deeply, their lungs unfettered. She'd name him Shaffer.

There were plenty of flyers left in the blue folder.

"Every day is spring, Mother."

She smiled. Her son was sweet. Incapable of being disingenuous. Was even loved within reason by the descendants of Charles and Leanna Hutchfield, Angela Carmen, Harper, Michael and Valerie, and had re-found Victor Robbins just to let him know he wasn't forgotten.

Plus, plus her son knew cousin Lewis' and Diane's offspring! But first Valerie had to get off the phone. Regina had the day off. Valerie, however, only got an hour for lunch, an hour quickly winding down.

Skillet and Shaffer would sit in the park called "Strawberry Fields" or "Lois Lanes" or maybe even "Idyll View" with the wind in the leaves and the wisped scents of flowers carried under their noses for just the merest hint of attention. "The dead guide us to seek their solace," Skillet said, making certain to catch the young man's eye, who was instead watching a fat bumblebee hovering at the grass.

"Death is immortality," the young man said.

"No shame in that," said Skillet. "No shame in dying."

"What about things left undone?"

Skillet scoffed. "Nothing is left undone. Future doesn't exist, boy."

The youth would call Skillet *Grandfather*.

"Grandfather—"

"Grandfather is tired. Watch the wind. Look for angels. Angels are folks who die in their sleep during dreams."

Moods and years change.

Dennis Sarantonio's lover, Dennis Grucci, died after three more winters. The service was beautiful. "I told him," Dennis said laughing through tears, "gay lovers never grow old...except the ones that wear ascots and don't have sex." He'd been caught by another bomb, but if it hadn't been the bomb it'd have been the random spray of bullets following it. This happened not more than half a block away from the relatively new park, which wasn't touched at all. Since there weren't as many deaths as there should have been, spring found more folks unconsciously gravitating toward Lois Lanes, eating, lounging, loafing in imagined safety.

Attendance reached the point that on any given day the park could nearly be seen from space. Families and loners sat everywhere, well-intentioned and considerate by huge silent agreement, as though to give in to incivility was tantamount to inviting wholesale bestiality (tapping along the fringes like a vampire at a window) to prowl their blankets and kite strings, feeding indiscriminately. Idiots even began to give a shit.

Happily, no one else died for quite some time. Terrorism fell briefly out of vogue, mainly because no one's ire honestly rose high enough to give glory and incentive to a bunch of tedius planning.

She was asleep and dreaming, elderly now, when she suddenly became aware of a lurching drop in consciousness. Pneumonia. Diagnosed too late. Hospitalized for four days, but in very little pain, and in remarkably good spirits. Everyone came to see her and told her she didn't look half as on display as she thought.

She couldn't open her eyelids to locate the source of that lurch but didn't worry either; inner sight sufficed. She waited patiently for the next lurch but was taken in a panic when it came, coming out of the darkness, soundless but so full of sensations. Mr. Bojangles frowned its little face in rapt concentration. Visiting hours were over. Even Dennis was gone. The skin of her lids danced. The mystery wanted to know what the dreams were and concentrated on her mind, but everything moved too quickly.

This time there was an angel, forming there in the corner. It smelled so good it almost broke the man-before's concentration. Heartening enough merely to know that this beauty had appeared, the most beautiful of fireflies.

Regina frowned. She felt old and realized she was. Distantly, she was aware of her body's heightened nudity courtesy the flimsy hospital gown, and knew that being so naked and exposed was in her secret heart a wonderful thing.

Something wanted her on the bottom of the ocean, down where living was a matter of electricity.

She slid quickly, feeling the rush of water around her.

Panic told her to grab onto things: everything about her, her fussy ways, her neglected Rosemary fingernails too much for a woman her age, the memories she retained of poems and affections, the way she walked, the emotional purpose of sex; all of her hairstyles, every stitch of clothing every year to every day of her life, every time she noticed a child who was cold and took a hesitant step to warm him before at some automatic signal the child unfailingly bolted away; the soft call of the wild whenever Dennis planted kisses on her hips, the way he tended her gardens now, the way she smiled, scratched the sides of her breasts, kept track of her debts, kept time with the usual people, the fact that she still had that library book, the weird one about the monkeys, with the preface that read, "Evolution does not follow any moral imperative." Even the memories other people had of her, especially memories, because death—and she realized these lurching drops of consciousness were death—death laid altered remembrances that erased *her* from the immediate world and made her cease to be who she'd been; she would become "Regina in death," forgiven and forgotten maybe.

Regina remembered dancing. When she danced it was in a way no one would admirably recognize as such. Sometimes, particularly summer nights which stretched as far as God could see, she forgot, and danced puttering with cleaning or if she couldn't sleep.

If the blackness swallowed her legs what would she do on long summer nights?

Lady sang the blues. The question had been where do people come from and where do they go? Now she knew they had always been there, even as fish with teeth and scales. People. Little nibbling people. Where they go is inside.

"Dear God. Father. Whatever. I'm not in any particular mood to be deferential to you. In fact, I'm here to make some demands." *I want to dance.*

Both were the beginnings of very appropriate prayers.

Give me more of God. I wait. I will not dream. I will not dream. The sun rises and I will not be. I will not see. I wait.

Why? And for what? Or whom.

Give me my lusts.

Give me the possibilities.

I will *not* wait for blind angels. Her wrinkled hand, in her sixty-third year, defiantly pulled the sheet closer to keep out a chill wind.

Dennis stared straight ahead. He felt uncomfortable. A woman outside had looked at him through a cloud of drugs and fog as though hard-pressed to accept his existence. Her short black outfit was stained and wrinkled.

"Mr. James?"

"Yes?"

"Don't be so tense."

Hard to shake. He talked.

"What have you seen that you weren't supposed to see?"

"Nothing yet," Shaffer said, peering intently into the other's face from behind the easel.

Sad, thought Dennis, but said nothing more. Young people should see things. Regina's call had set this in motion. Dennis had never sat still without need for the usual worries or escapes long enough for an artist to capture him. He didn't worry that he might appear unattractive or hardly worthy of a portrait, he worried about the forest. It hadn't seemed proper to tell Shaffer how to treat his subject.

And he hadn't.

So he had no idea where he was on the canvas, or how he looked. The only thing he knew was where he hoped to be. Regina had been drawn into a forest; he wanted to be there too. He imagined the richest smells he'd never experienced and a gentle sun. Common enough.

He sat fully clothed on Shaffer's sofa, his hands in his lap.

After a while his mind turned inward to thoughts of the blue folder Regina watched over, and the automaton scritch scratch of Shaffer's sketching hand knifing across the page.

The boy looked tired and hungry.

"Rest if you need to." *Don't look so sad.*

"I'll stop when I get hungry."

Made in the USA
Monee, IL
11 May 2021